The Field of Wacky Inventions

BOOK THREE

The Field of Wacky Inventions

by Patrick Carman

SCHOLASTIC INC.

This book was originally published in hardcover by Scholastic Press in 2013.

ISBN 978-0-545-79859-4

12 11 10 9 8 7 6 5 4 3 2 1 15 16 17 18 19 20/0

Printed in the U.S.A. 40

First printing 2015

The text type was set in Revival 565 BT.
Book design by Christopher Stengel

For Susan Schulman.

Merganzer, Leo, and Remi are very lucky to call her friend. And so am I.

For where your treasure is,
there will your heart be also.

— *Matthew 6:21*

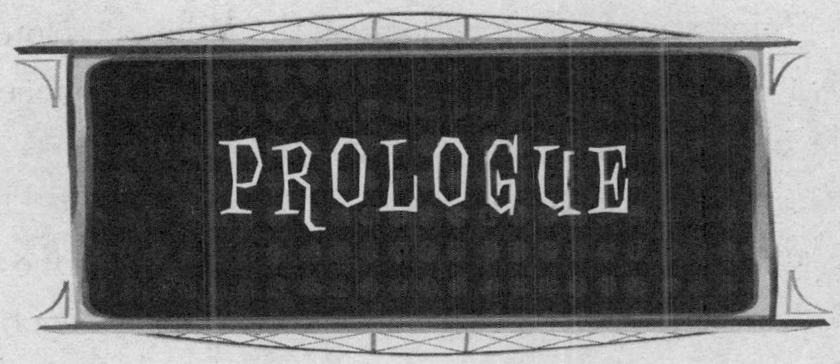

"Is that you?"

"Of course it's me. Who else would it be?"

"You won't believe where I am."

"It's been a trying day; could you make this quick?"

Ms. Sparks, who had been foiled again and again by Merganzer D. Whippet, had indeed endured a very bad day. Her plan to take over the Whippet Hotel had failed for a second time, and her prospects were extremely dim.

"The top floor of my hotel just took off into the air," Ms. Sparks was told. "An airship is carrying it away. Very odd."

Ms. Sparks sat up straight on her ratty old couch, where she had been dozing as the television droned in the background.

"Are you on board?" she asked.

"I was just getting to that," the voice stammered, surprised by the fact that Ms. Sparks actually believed the top of a hotel had been lifted into the air. "I'm standing on the roof."

"Interesting. The top floor of the Whippet Hotel has also gone missing. And you have the satellite phone? The one that skips all the cell towers?"

"Of course. I'm using it now."

Ms. Sparks tried to imagine what kind of madness Merganzer was cooking up and how she might benefit from it.

"Call me when you land. Let's see where this little adventure leads us."

"Understood."

"And one more thing," Ms. Sparks warned. "If you find two kids along the way, keep an eye on them. They're not as dumb as they look. I have a feeling they hold the keys to Merganzer's kingdom."

When the call was completed, Ms. Sparks rose from the couch and tamed her beehive hair, which was tilted to the side like the Leaning Tower of Pisa.

She took a single hard cookie from the battered coffee table and crushed it into dust.

"What are you up to, Merganzer D. Whippet?"

· CHAPTER 1 ·

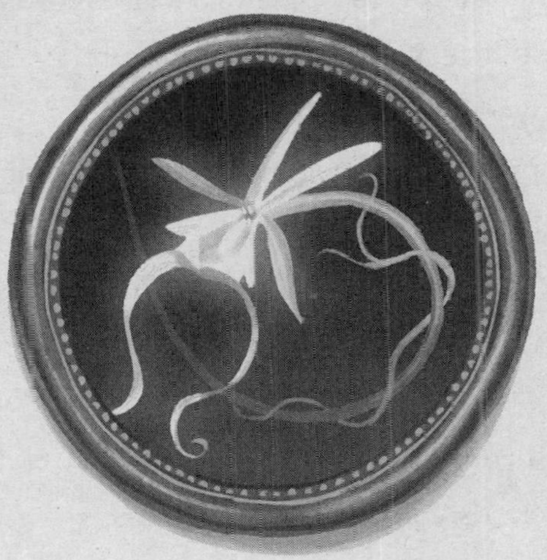

IT BEGAN WITH A LETTER

Clarence and Pilar Fillmore didn't even have time to drop their bags on the floor of the lobby before surprising things began happening at the Whippet Hotel. It had been a long travel day and they'd arrived home late. They'd expected to see no one until morning, but Captain Rickenbacker was sliding down the banister, wearing his red cape, which flapped in the breeze behind him. It felt very much like he'd been waiting for the door of the hotel to open so he could descend on an unsuspecting visitor.

When Captain Rickenbacker arrived at the bottom of the stairs, he produced a white envelope from his vest pocket.

"This came for you in the afternoon post."

He said the words like they were part of a grand conspiracy.

"Hello, Captain Rickenbacker," Clarence said. "It's nice to see you, too."

"It's from *him*."

"Him? Who is *him*?" Pilar asked. She had the most charming Mexican accent Clarence Fillmore had ever heard — he never grew tired of hearing it — but Captain Rickenbacker's voice was all business.

"There is only one him — *the* him," Captain Rickenbacker said.

Pilar looked at Clarence, puzzled but amused. She loved all the quirky people who lived in the Whippet Hotel.

"Merganzer D. Whippet," Clarence said, for there really was only one *him* in their world, it was true.

"Of course. What was I thinking?" Pilar said, batting her deep brown eyes in the direction of the envelope as she gently removed it from Captain Rickenbacker's hand.

The captain fluffed his cape and turned to go, then looked back and added one more piece of information he'd nearly forgotten to share.

"Oh, and the top of the hotel has vanished. I'm investigating."

Clarence should have been highly alarmed, but he was used to the extraordinary goings-on at the hotel. He took it in stride.

"Where are Leo and Remi?" Mr. Fillmore asked.

But Captain Rickenbacker was already leaving, on his way back up the stairs in the direction of the Pinball Machine, where he solved crimes and ate donuts. He was not one to dawdle after a mission had been completed.

"Better read it," Pilar said, stepping out of her sandals. She liked the feel of the cool marble floor on the bottoms of her feet.

And so Clarence popped the wax seal on the envelope, removed the letter, and read it out loud.

Clarence and Pilar,

Welcome home! I trust you had a marvelous time on your honeymoon in the Riviera. You have been missed!

Things have been quiet as usual in your absence. Humdrum, dull, a real snooze. The boys were practically dying of boredom, so I decided to intervene on their behalf.

I hope you won't mind that I've taken them on a little adventure. Nothing too exciting. There will be a lot of naps and checkers, that sort of thing.

Take good care of the hotel in their absence. I'll have them back in a week.

With fondness on your return,
Merganzer D. Whippet

The truth, of course, was there had been no humdrum, no dull, no snoozing at the Whippet Hotel while Pilar and Clarence had been away. Leo and Remi had been in the vast underbelly of the hotel most of the time, searching through a hidden jungle, a mad scientist's underground laboratory, and the realm of gears, which had all been every bit as dangerous as it sounds.

Pilar shrugged. Though she still had a bride's glow about her, she was also exhausted from all the traveling.

"It's Merganzer. How dangerous could it be?" she asked.

But Clarence knew better. *A little adventure* could mean almost anything when it came to Merganzer D. Whippet. At least Leo and Remi were smart, resourceful, and careful.

"They'll be fine," he said with a half smile, for he was only half sure. "How about we start our week by getting some sleep?"

If only they'd known how Leo and Remi's little adventure was beginning, the last thing on their minds would have been turning in for the night.

· CHAPTER 2 ·

LAND HO!

Leo and Remi were on the roof that had gone missing from the Whippet Hotel. The entire top floor of the Whippet was flying through the sky, held aloft by a vast and nearly invisible airship. That alone should have been enough to make them both dizzy with anticipation, but really, it was only the beginning.

They were moving quietly above a low blanket of clouds. Looking down made Leo feel safe, as though the clouds were a soft bed of cotton candy the top of the Whippet Hotel could land on if the airship overhead failed them. If he could have seen how high they really were, it would have taken his breath away.

"Where are we going?" Remi asked for the tenth time. "And when will we get there?"

Mr. Powell was above them in the cockpit of the blimp, guiding them to places unknown, but everyone else, including Merganzer, had gone down to the roof below. Merganzer wouldn't stop playing with the ducks. He sat cross-legged by the small pond, letting the new ducklings climb into his lap. One had long fallen asleep in his hand, and he cupped it like a delicate egg, watching as it breathed a hundred breaths a minute.

"Let's call this one Comet," Merganzer said. He brushed a finger across the strip of yellow-white fur running along the duckling's back. "He's going to be a fast one, I can tell."

"I don't know," Leo said as he and Remi came close. "Maybe we should call him Snoozy instead."

"He's saving his energy," Merganzer replied. "For when he really needs it."

"So about that destination," said Remi. "And when we're getting there?"

Comet woke with a start, his little eyes blinking wildly. He jumped out of Merganzer's hand, racing for the pond. The white strip of fur down his back did look kind of like a comet streaking across the sky.

"You see there? He *is* fast!"

Remi went back to looking at the clouds below them, resting his elbows on the wide rail of the Whippet Hotel roof. Leo and Merganzer joined Remi, and the three of them stared out into the starry night, an icy wind blowing through their hair.

"How about we look over this way, shall we?" Merganzer said. He opened up his long coat and wrapped the boys in its warmth, pulling them along as they flew across the night sky. Merganzer was nearing his fiftieth birthday, but he had the wondrous heart of a boy leaving on an adventure.

"There, can you see it now?" he asked. Merganzer pointed out with a finger that was almost as crooked as his long nose was. "Way off in the distance."

They'd long left the lights of the city behind, and the clouds below had turned black and forbidding. But Merganzer D. Whippet wasn't pointing at the clouds, he was looking across the sky, where something was coming toward them. At nearly twelve years old, Remi and Leo had never known stars to shine so brightly, because they'd both been city dwellers their entire lives. They turned their gazes away from the sparkling sky above and followed the line of Merganzer's finger.

"Looks like a hot dog," Remi said. He was a semiround boy who thought about food a great deal of the time.

"Wait, that's —" Leo began to say, and Remi jumped in.

"It is! It is a giant hot dog!"

Leo rolled his eyes, something he found himself doing quite a lot when he was with his newly acquired stepbrother. "It's not a hot dog. It's an airship."

"I'm sorry to disappoint you, Remi," Merganzer said. "But Leo is right. And that's not the only one."

The flying thing off in the distance did have the shape of a hot dog. A *huge* hot dog. It turned slowly, like a submarine in the ocean, and headed straight for the roof of the Whippet Hotel.

"Hey, there's another one!" Remi yelled, and he ran from under the cover of Merganzer's long coat, pointing his pudgy finger toward an approaching light.

"What's going on here?" Leo asked as he turned toward Merganzer. He was a boy with a bubble of curly hair, which raked forward into his bright eyes as the wind pushed against the back of his head.

"Just watch," said their mystifying companion. "I bet you'll figure it out on your own."

And so they did.

Airships were coming in from all directions, and they were all on a path pointing toward one another, as if a funnel in the middle of the sky was pulling them closer. Like the blimp that floated over Leo's head, these approaching airships were also carrying cargo.

"Wait, are those what I think they are?" Leo asked, leaning as far out over the ledge of the Whippet Hotel roof as he dared. There were five airships — six including the one over Leo's head — and all of them were carrying something.

Leo turned to Merganzer and stared up into his twinkling eyes.

"How many hotels do you own?" Leo asked.

Merganzer's eyes darted back and forth, as if he'd been caught with a secret.

"More than one."

Leo returned his gaze to the ledge, where the five other balloons were getting awfully close to one another. Each of them carried the roof of a different hotel.

"This is outrageous," Remi said to Merganzer. "Even for you."

"Why, thank you, Remi. That means a lot."

Leo couldn't take his eyes off the scene unfolding before him. The airships had come to a stop. They were like floating centurions, staring silently at one another in a circle. Looking more carefully, Leo thought he saw people standing on the roofs of the buildings.

"Who are they?" Leo asked. "And why did you bring them up here?"

But Merganzer only smiled broadly, looking out at the tops of all his hotels as they floated in front of him.

Blop, Remi's miniature robot, peeked his head out from Remi's pocket and observed the approaching vessels with some interest.

"Airships are marvelous inventions, especially good for carrying heavy loads a long way," he began. Once Blop started in on a subject it was hard to get him to stop. He went on about the crash of the mighty *Hindenburg,* which had put an end to the use of hydrogen inside of airships.

"Also called zeppelins, because they were originally invented by Count Zeppelin, and later, in World War I, blimps — but the source of the word *blimp* is unknown."

The boys watched all the airships move toward them as Blop went on and on about how the flying vessels were normally filled with helium, which made them lighter than air and gave them their ability to float. It was here that Merganzer interjected.

"You'll be pleased to know I've done some reengineering. The stuff I put in these airships is much more powerful than plain old helium. Also a tad unstable, but nothing to worry about. As long as we don't unhook the weights unexpectedly, we'll be fine."

"The weights?" Remi asked.

"I think he's referring to the top of the Whippet Hotel," Leo said.

"So right!" Merganzer said, slapping Leo on the back with a gloved hand. "Now that we're hooked up, we need to stay hooked up. Unhooking is a delicate process."

"What would happen if the zip rope snapped?" Leo asked. The zip rope was made from a very special monkey tail. It has amazing strength, like a million rubber bands all wrapped together.

"A zip rope break?" Merganzer asked. "Why, that's impossible! But since you asked, I'll tell you. We would fall — I suppose that much is perfectly clear. But the airship overhead, it would fall, too. Only it would fall *up*. Up, up, up it would go as fast as we would fall. And it wouldn't stop until it reached the moon."

"Cool," Remi said. He could imagine a blimp slamming into the moon in a ball of fire.

"If my calculations are correct," Blop said, "it would appear that we're beginning our descent."

"What's that supposed to mean?" Remi asked.

"It means we're finally landing!" Leo said excitedly,

and as he said the words, all six hotel roofs drifted down and vanished into thick clouds. Everything turned hazy and soft around the edges as beams of light from the airships darted in every direction. And then, without any warning at all, the roof of the Whippet Hotel burst through the clouds and the ground appeared below them. Darkness lay for miles in every direction, and in the center of all that darkness, Merganzer D. Whippet's estate sat quietly waiting for them.

The first time Leo and Remi saw the field of wacky inventions, they both knew it would forever remain one of the most magical moments of their lives. Even after everything they'd seen inside the Whippet Hotel and the many adventures they'd had, they both knew this place was something special.

"Getting close, sir," Mr. Powell yelled down from the airship cockpit. "Better turn on the lights!"

Merganzer's eyebrows raised in anticipation and he took a hotel key card out of his coat pocket. Leo and Remi watched as he swiped his finger across the face of the card, then touched the top of the card and ran his finger slowly down the middle. Down below, two curved strips of light appeared and inside the strips, the letters began to appear.

W H I P P E T

The letters must have been twenty feet wide, for the airship was still high up in the air and the word was bright and clear. Merganzer tapped his finger on the key card over and over, and down below glowing circles of light appeared around the WHIPPET. Six round circles of light shone up through a field of wide oak trees, making the leaves glow bright red and yellow like a forest afire.

"Landing locations illuminated!" Merganzer shouted up to Mr. Powell.

There was enough light now for Leo and Remi to see the outline of the entire world they were about to enter. From overhead, they could see the tops of the great oak trees, their canopies hiding whatever lay hidden beneath. There were openings for the airships to dock, and a high stone wall wrapped around the entire property, encasing everything in secrecy.

"So this is the field of wacky inventions," Leo said.

"Looks awesome," Remi said.

"You have no idea," Merganzer replied, then he leapt up onto the edge of the narrow rail that ran around the roof of the Whippet Hotel.

"I'm just a kid," Remi said. "But I think that's a bad idea."

"Land ho!" Merganzer yelled, ignoring Remi as he leaned over the edge of the Whippet Hotel in a most precarious fashion. Leo and Remi each grabbed one side of his coat, trying to hold his tall frame steady as Merganzer wobbled back and forth, shuffled unsteadily to the left, and fell off the roof. Merganzer's coat slipped off quietly as he fell, and Leo and Remi each held one empty sleeve as they looked at each other and screamed.

"Don't worry too much, boys," Mr. Powell said. "Merganzer usually has a plan even I don't know about."

Sure enough, a parachute popped open and they watched as Merganzer drifted below them, expertly navigating a path to the very circle of light Leo and Remi were headed for. By the time they arrived in their airship, Merganzer had landed, moved out of the way, and stood waiting.

"What took you so long?" Merganzer said, laughing up at Mr. Powell as the roof of the Whippet Hotel touched down.

"Can't talk now, need to land more airships!" Mr. Powell said.

Mr. Powell carefully moved each of the other five buildings into position, controlling the airships from inside the cockpit. If Leo and Remi could have seen the control panel Mr. Powell was in command of, its complexity would have made them marvel with delight.

"This is turning out to be a very weird night," Remi said as other hotel roofs settled into place with a hiss of steam on lighted pads. Underfoot, a clatter of mechanical sounds led Leo to believe the top of the Whippet Hotel would forever after be something else. It was being bolted into place on the ground, where the Whippet was bound to stay. Its days of grandeur at the top of a building had, it seemed, come to an end.

There were wide tree trunks and tangled limbs everywhere, but Remi and Leo could see around those things as the other five floors settled into place across the grounds. Leo had a keen sense of observation, and he found it curious that none of the other floors landed with an array of mechanical sounds. Gazing up into the trees, Leo saw strange, unexplainable tracks running everywhere. Vines hung from the great oaks, and, pushing a few of them to the side, Remi looked up and saw one of the airships hovering quietly overhead like a parent watching his or her children in a new and dangerous place.

"Hey, Blop," Remi said, pulling the robot out of his pocket so he could have a good look around. "What can you tell us about this place?"

Blop spun around two or three times, made some important-sounding whirs and beeps, and answered: "Number of spiders in the immediate vicinity: between twelve thousand and two million. Odds of having one crawl into your mouth if we sleep outside tonight: fifty-fifty."

"That was *so* unhelpful," Remi said, gulping as he imagined a spider crawling down his throat.

"I'm not that useful after midnight," Blop explained in his tinny voice. "Low energy."

Remi put Blop back in his pocket and shook his head.

"Weird robot," Leo said.

"You're telling me. I live with the guy. You should hear some of the predictions he gives me in the middle of the night. Did you know the odds of finding a snake in your bed at some point in your life are —"

"Stop!" Leo said, putting his hand up in Remi's face. "I don't want to know."

"One in nine," Blop said from Remi's pocket, his mechanical voice all muffled and faraway-sounding.

Leo couldn't believe they'd gotten into such a meaningless conversation. Nor could he fathom the terrible odds he'd just been given about snakes and spiders in the night. While Leo thought about these things, an army of orange-tailed monkeys descended from the trees. They slid down a long orange zip rope attached to a golden duck at the center of the roof.

"Hey! It's the same kind of guys as under the hotel back home!" Remi said. "Cool."

Leo and Remi watched as the Leprechaun monkeys began untying all the ropes that held the airship to the roof of the Whippet Hotel.

"Looks like we might be staying awhile," Leo said, taking notice as each rope came untied. Only the center line — the orange zip rope — remained. It had once been a monkey's tail, but now it was just another of Merganzer D. Whippet's outrageous inventions: the strongest rope in the world, strong enough to pick up a building or lasso a whale.

"Leo!"

Mr. Powell was leaning out from the cab above, staring down at the boys.

"You'll have to do the last part. Use these!"

Mr. Powell tossed something out of the sky. It missed the pond by only a foot, landing with a thud on the green grass of the hotel roof.

"Quickly now," Mr. Powell said. "Untie the zip rope! I've made all the preparations for takeoff."

Mr. Powell vanished for a moment, then he was back, leaning down and yelling.

"I'm off on a supply run. Quickly now, Leo. Untie me!"

Leo picked up the strangest set of pliers he'd ever seen. They had four prongs that came together when the handles were squeezed. Leo tried them and the four prongs set off sparks at the center.

"Whoa. That's a mean set of pliers you got there," Remi said. "I bet they'd work on a snake in your bed. I'll give you a dollar for them."

Leo loved tools of every kind and kept many of them in his maintenance overalls. He was thrilled to have such a rare and unusual pair of pliers. The golden duck was in the center of the pond, but the monkeys had all made a chain overhead that ran from one side of the building to the other, right over the center of the water, wrapping their limbs together. One of them reached down and grabbed Leo by the back of his maintenance overalls and picked him up, passing him along the chain of monkeys.

"On my way!" Leo yelled up to Mr. Powell.

"So I see." Mr. Powell laughed.

While Leo made his way to the zip rope on a chain of orange-tailed monkeys, Merganzer D. Whippet suddenly appeared next to Remi.

"He's doing quite well, wouldn't you say?"

Remi was so taken by surprise he nearly jumped out of his bellboy jacket.

"You shouldn't sneak up on people like that. I thought you were a snake."

"The snakes around here are very quiet. You wouldn't know they were close until it was too late."

"Sometimes it's better if you don't share *everything*."

Merganzer chuckled softly. He retrieved his coat, which had come off when he'd gone skydiving.

"My dear boy, I'm only telling a tall tale. There are no snakes here. The spiders are *huge*, but no snakes. I promise."

"Okay, ready?" Leo yelled. He'd arrived at the golden duck, where the orange zip rope was tightly tied in place.

"Untie it!" Merganzer yelled back.

Leo turned around and smiled at Merganzer, then looked up at Mr. Powell just to be sure. Mr. Powell gave a thumbs-up, but when he leaned over the edge of the cab this time, he was wearing a big, goofy helmet and racing goggles.

"Ready!" he said.

"Why's he wearing a helmet?" Remi asked Merganzer.

Merganzer shook his head as if telling Remi he shouldn't worry, everything was going to be fine. "Take-off can be a little bit unstable."

Leo reached down and put the four prongs around the zip-rope knot and pressed the handles together. Sparks flew and the pliers jumped in Leo's hand, like he'd just sent a jolt of electricity through the knot. He watched, but the knot didn't move.

"Turn it up to ten and hit it again!" Merganzer said.

Leo examined the pliers more carefully and found a round dial at the end of one of the handles. There were ten small numbers on the face of the dial, and it was currently set to number 2.

"Are you sure we should go straight to ten?" Leo asked.

"Oh yes, definitely go for the gusto," Merganzer said. Mr. Powell looked down, and though the goggles hid part of his round face, Remi was pretty sure Mr. Powell was alarmed.

When Leo had clicked the dial eight times and it was set at a whopping number 10, he took a deep breath and held the four prongs over the knot.

"We should probably stand back," Merganzer said, putting a hand against Remi's red jacket and pushing him toward the rail of the Whippet Hotel.

"What about Leo?" Remi asked, scared for his brother, who was hanging right over the top of the knot.

Merganzer didn't have time to answer before Leo pressed the handles together and the four metal prongs delivered a mega-sized shot of electricity. Leo and the monkeys were blown back as though they'd bounced off a gigantic trampoline. The sky filled with monkeys, flipping and turning in every direction, while Leo went airborne thirty feet over the Whippet Hotel.

"Leo!" Remi yelled. His little bellboy cap had been blown off and his jacket buttons had burst open from the impact, but he didn't care about any of that. His brother was in real trouble . . . or so he thought.

The monkeys began to catch one another's hands, forming a long chain that ran from thick tree limbs above out into the night sky. Two of them — just to be extra safe — had hold of Leo's maintenance overalls, and soon it was clear that Leo was getting the ride of his life. He swayed back and forth on a string of monkeys, laughing and acting like an airplane as he flew back and forth.

"How come he gets to have all the fun?" Remi asked.

"Well, he does own the hotel," Merganzer said, putting a hand on Remi's shoulder. "And he's very handy."

Remi looked down at his hands and remembered that he was often fumble-fingered when it came to delicate tasks.

"You picked the right guy for the job."

The monkeys set Leo down on the roof and retreated up into the trees, where they sat watching the airship. The zip rope hadn't come untied, but the knot was loosening ever so slowly.

"That was quite a jolt," Leo said. "Maybe next time you could warn me."

"If you'd known, you'd never have done it," Merganzer said. "That's a life lesson worth noting."

Merganzer knelt down and looked at the two boys. "Life is full of adventures we'd never take if we knew how they were going to turn out before we did them. But we're always better for having had the courage to *live*. Understand?"

Both boys did understand. They'd spent enough time in Merganzer's world to have already learned the lesson. Would they have ever ventured under the Whippet Hotel if they'd known how dangerous it would be? Certainly not! But looking back, they'd never, ever want to have missed meeting Clyde, the mechanical dog, or Dr. Flart, or Loopa the monkey. If they'd known the danger that lurked below — the atomic ants, the realm of gears — they would have been too afraid. But then they'd never have burped after a Flart's Fizz or enjoyed the amazing grape flavor of foamy Flooooog.

The boys were thinking of all those adventures, wishing they could do them all again, when the knot on the zip rope finally popped free with a loud *snap*!

"And he's off!" Merganzer said, standing and turning his head skyward. The airship shot into the air, rising like a rocket taking off for the moon. Merganzer took a key card out of his coat and pressed the screen.

"Everything all right, George?"

Mr. Powell's distant voice returned: "All systems go! Stabilizing!"

"Excellent! Make sure to bring more pickles," Merganzer said. "And onion rings."

"Check!" Mr. Powell said. "Will be back in a few days!"

Merganzer smiled down at Leo and Remi, putting a hand on each shoulder as Betty and her little ducklings came near. She was quacking angrily, like all the commotion had woken her up.

"Never wake a duck," Merganzer said. "They hold a grudge."

"Noted," Remi said as the duckling Merganzer had named Comet pecked at his shoe.

"It's been a long night," Merganzer said with a sigh. "Time to get some sleep. Tomorrow morning, all will be revealed!"

Before either of the boys could reply, a tiny monkey with an orange tail landed on Remi's shoulder and he turned to look at it. "Why am I not surprised?"

There was a monkey on Leo's shoulder, too, and suddenly the two boys were being hoisted into the sky on their way to a tree house, where they would spend a quiet night among the monkeys.

Little did they know that a competition was already afoot, one that would require all their skills and every bit of courage they could muster.

The biggest adventure of them all was about to arrive in the field of wacky inventions.

• CHAPTER 3 •

WHAT THEY FOUND BEYOND THE WALL

Leo woke to the gurgling hum of Remi's breathing at the crack of dawn. At first he mistook the sound for the basement boiler at the Whippet Hotel, but sitting up and looking from side to side, he realized he was no longer in the great city of Manhattan. Blue sky peeked through the canopy of limbs and leaves overhead. Standing up, Leo investigated the three rooms of the small tree house: a bathroom (he stopped in for a little visit); a sitting room, with a table holding a bowl of bright green apples (he took one and bit into it); and the sleeping porch, with its two hammocks (one nearly touched the floor under the weight of his stepbrother).

Instead of waking up Remi, Leo crept past the sagging hammock and went outside with his crunchy apple. A catwalk with a rail made of tree limbs ran a circle around the tree house, and Leo walked the whole way around, trying to get a good look at the ground below. The tracks he'd barely been able to see the night before looped and twirled in parallel sets between the giant oaks. But they were hard to see even in the morning light, because the rails looked more like tree limbs and roots than any sort of track something might ride on. Leo was way up in the tree, far enough that much of the world he now found himself in remained a mystery, hidden behind leaves and limbs. He could see some tents and a long, angular building painted with polka dots, and he could see the far edge of the wall in one spot, but that was about it. When he looked straight up, he saw a series of wood slats nailed to the side of the tree, leading to a platform even higher still.

Leo finished his apple and tossed the core out into the open space below the tree, but before it could hit the ground, not one but four monkeys had either grabbed it or were trying to steal it from one another. They made a lot of noise, which finally woke up Remi.

"What a racket," Remi said, stumbling out onto the porch, barely awake. "Any food around here?"

"In there, on the table," Leo said as he took an inventory of his maintenance overalls. He couldn't quite remember all that he'd brought, and it had occurred to him on waking that tools could be very important in a place like this. Remi came alongside, eating an apple.

"You didn't by any chance bring a candy bar, did you?" he asked, making a sour face at the tart flavor of the one thing they had to eat. "This thing tastes like monkey food."

One of the guiding principles of the universe is that you don't have to tell a monkey twice that you're holding monkey food. The words were barely out of Remi's mouth when the apple was snatched out of his hand and fought over by more squealing monkeys.

"I have those crazy pliers Mr. Powell threw down to me," Leo said, starting to pull things out and put them back into his many pockets one by one. "And I brought some other stuff that might be useful: half a roll of duct tape, a Swiss Army knife, a rock hammer, a ball of string, and three pennies. Oh, and some beef jerky, but it's been in here for about a year. None of that really helps us figure out what to do next, does it?"

"I only brought a robot," Remi responded, swiping the beef jerky with noticeable excitement.

Remi pulled Blop out of his pocket and held him at arm's length as his eyes opened up.

"You shouldn't hold me this way," Blop said. "I could fall."

Blop began to explain what would happen if he were dropped from a high distance — what it could do to his memory chip, how delicate his wiring was, and so on. The best thing to do when Blop talked about something no one cared about was to point his attention toward something else. He was highly distractible.

"My guess is you were invented here," Remi said. "Got any memories about *that*?"

Blop's little head whirled back and forth and he made a lot of goofy beeping sounds. "There are dangerous things down there," Blop said. "Better stay up here, where it's safe. But if you must go down there — *highly* unwise — you can use the zip lines."

"Why'd you have to go and say that?" Remi tried to say, for he hated zip lines. But his mouth was full of linty, dry beef jerky, so instead it sounded like *fwy chew haffa go a shay sat?*

"This is not a language I know," Blop said in reply. "Is it Yeti?"

After that there was no use with Blop. He hated not knowing the answer to things and became highly annoying whenever it happened. Remi rolled his eyes and put Blop back in his jacket pocket.

"Up there!" Leo said. He'd already spied a long row of tree limbs nailed to the side of the tree leading overhead to a platform. "Come on! We can get down there before anyone wakes up and have a look around."

"And why would we want to do that?"

Remi had managed, with great effort, to swallow the beef jerky. It was wholly unsatisfying.

"Wait for me!" he yelled up, because Leo knew there was one thing Remi hated more than riding zip lines: getting left behind.

When the two boys arrived on the platform, they found it considerably less stable than they'd hoped it would be. It wobbled in the soft morning breeze blowing through the limbs, and there were no rails whatsoever. Just a flat place to stand, a wooden box of rollers for riding on, and a long zip line that ended someplace they couldn't see.

"Remember how we used these before?" Leo asked. "Under the Whippet Hotel, in the underground jungle?"

"I remember it was not enjoyable," said Remi. "Especially the landing part."

"Come on — it'll be fun," Leo said. "I bet there are pancakes down there."

Remi's eyes lit up. The beef jerky had tasted like dirt, and he knew Merganzer was famous for cooking up breakfasts that were super-amazing, fantastic, and great.

"You had me at pancakes," Remi said. "Let's do this."

They each picked up one of the rollers, and Leo set his over the top of the rigid line. "Follow me. I'll yell back if there are any obstacles."

"Obstacles? Who said anything about obstacles?"

Before Remi could change his mind about the whole endeavor, Leo dove off the platform and into the air, zipping down the line, away from the tree house. Remi followed a little too close, and because he was heavier, caught up to Leo in approximately two seconds.

"Incoming!" Remi screamed, plowing into Leo's back and sending him twisting and turning as they approached a wide limb in their path. Leo barely lifted his legs in time.

"Lift your legs, Remi! Quick!"

Remi did as he was told, but he was quite a bit shorter than Leo, so he hadn't needed to lift his legs. Forming into a cannonball did make him go faster, though, and he clobbered Leo again as they both screamed and careened down the zip line toward a platform in the middle of the outer wall. The line leveled out as they approached the end, and Leo was able to hop off and stand upright, the wall around the field of wacky inventions staring him in the face. Remi came in like a bowling ball, toppling Leo like a pin and slamming into the stone wall.

"Whose idea was this again?" Remi said as he shook his head.

"I guess that would be me. Sorry, bro," Leo offered. He was rubbing his side, where he'd just been struck by a Remi wrecking ball.

The platform was right in the center of the wall — no closer to the ground than the top edge of the stones.

"Looks like it's about twenty feet up there," Leo said.

"And twenty feet down," Remi said. He was looking down into a hole on the platform that had a ladder leading to the ground.

"Let's have a look outside first, shouldn't we?" Leo asked. "We can go down right after."

Remi sniffed the air.

"Someone's cooking," he said, standing up. He sniffed some more, like a dog on a scent, and pointed back in the direction from which they'd come. "Down there. It's bacon."

"Just give me two seconds," Leo pleaded. "Don't you want to know where we are?"

Remi looked up, then back in the direction of the unseen bacon sizzling on a grill, then at his stepbrother and best friend in the whole world.

"You're the only person I'd do this for, but okay. Let's get up there and have a look."

Leo smiled broadly and the two began climbing. A ladder leading up the side of the wall was wide enough for both of them to ascend side by side, so they went together. Remi kept looking over his shoulder, in search of breakfast, but there were so many branches and vines and tree trunks, it was useless. He could barely see past his own nose, let alone all the way off into the field of wacky inventions.

"They sure do know how to grow trees around this place."

It was farther than either of them had supposed when they had looked up, and the rungs were farther apart the higher they climbed. By the time they reached up and touched the top of the wall, they were both out of breath.

"This thing is wider than I expected it to be," Leo said, ever the observer of all things before him. The top of the wall was about three feet wide, so both boys hopped up on top and let their legs dangle down on the other side.

"Merganzer D. Whippet is a strange dude," Remi said. "The guy's got a moat."

Hazy green water came right to the edge of the wall and spanned fifty feet across. It was so wide, the moat made the field of wacky inventions look like it was sitting in the middle of a lake.

"Do you suppose there are any alligators in there?" Remi asked, flipping over onto his stomach and lying down on the wall with his face staring down at the water.

"One way to find out," Leo answered, pulling out another lint-covered piece of beef jerky and tossing it over the edge of the wall. He reclined next to Remi and waited as the jerky floated on the surface of the water like a piece of bark from a tree. Looking past the moat, Leo saw a vast space of empty land, presumably owned by Merganzer, and no sign of a road into the property anywhere. It would seem that the only way in was by airship.

"Check it out," Remi said. "Did you see that?"

Leo snapped to attention and looked straight down at the beef jerky. There were swirling movements coming in from four directions, and while Leo looked, four alligator heads burst out of the water and went after the treat at once. The water turned into a frothing, churning sea of sharp teeth and slapping tails.

"I think I've seen enough," Remi said, sitting up and looking back into the relative calm of the world inside the walls. "Let's go get breakfast."

Leo had to agree — there wasn't a whole lot more

sitting on top of the wall was going to get them. They'd gotten about as much information as they were likely to get, and it was not good: They were isolated, there was no way out, and there were alligators in the moat.

Whatever Merganzer D. Whippet was doing in the field of wacky inventions, he didn't want anyone finding out about it.

"Come on," Remi said. "There's nothing a good pancake won't make better. Let's go find out what's going on around here."

• CHAPTER 4 •

THE GAME IS AFOOT

It was easy finding their way back. All they had to do was climb down onto the ground and follow the smell of sizzling bacon, which became stronger and more pleasant the closer they got to its source. As they walked, they saw enormous round tents and oddly shaped buildings off in the distance between the trees, but they didn't dare do any more exploring on their own without permission. If there were alligators in the moat, there was no telling what might be lurking in a structure that looked like a circus tent.

"It looks like the other airships are still here," Leo said as they passed near a square building sitting on the grass with ropes leading up into the tall trees. "I think ours was the only one that took off last night."

"And we've arrived," Remi said as they walked under a circle of leafy tree limbs overhead. Bright green grass covered a small grove they'd found, and in the middle, a long stone table awaited them. It appeared, from the way everyone was staring at them, that they were late.

"Is this them?"

The voice was not friendly, and the face that delivered it was even less so. It belonged to a man dressed in a white suit, with the longest face Leo had ever seen in his life, made longer because of the pointed white beard that extended six inches off his chin.

Merganzer was standing to the side, wearing an apron and a tall hat. He presided over a round cooking surface as big as a tractor tire. When he saw Leo and Remi, he lit up like a Christmas tree.

"There you are! I was starting to wonder who was going to eat all these pancakes. Have a seat — we've been expecting you."

There were five people seated at the long table, and they all looked as if they'd not only already eaten but had also grown tired of waiting around for whatever was going to come next. Leo and Remi sat down in the two empty chairs and waited for their pancakes and bacon to arrive. The plates before them were more like pizza pie pans — huge — and this made both of them feel a tinge of excitement in their empty stomachs.

"Where have you been hiding?" a meticulously dressed, overly tanned woman with jet-black hair asked. She was more Hollywood than Fifth Avenue, and Leo had the feeling she was much older than she appeared. Had he been aware of all the ways in which a person could hold back the sands of time, at least in the facial department, he would have been doubly sure she was pushing seventy even if she didn't look a day over forty.

"We were up in a tree house," Remi said. "It took some work getting down here."

The woman introduced herself as Miss Harrington, then picked up her coffee cup and stared off into the trees. Leo had the distinct feeling something was going on here that he wasn't fully in on, but there was no way to be sure. He didn't have time to think more about it because Merganzer had sprung into action.

"Incoming!" he shouted, flipping a pancake the size of a dinner plate into the air and over the long table. The pancake flew skyward, rolling end over end as it went, and arrived in the general vicinity over Leo's and Remi's heads. Leo was fast, but Remi was faster. Before Leo knew it, Remi had his gigantic plate held high in the air, catching the pancake before Leo could get under it.

"Nice catch," Leo had to admit.

Remi sniffed the pancake and his dark eyebrows rose. "He cooked the bacon right into this thing. By golly, he *is* a genius."

"Incoming!" Merganzer screamed again, and a second unusually large pancake went flying and flipping.

"I do wish he would stop shouting," a dapper-looking gentleman at the end of the long table said. He rested his chin on the end of a long cane, which had a golden duck head for a top.

"I got this one!" Leo cried, and he did, standing up and holding his plate higher than Remi could reach (a good thing, because Remi was shamelessly going for two out of two).

Merganzer walked to the head of the table, where Leo and Remi sat on his left, and pulled what looked like a can of spray paint out of his apron pocket.

"Whipped cream," Remi whispered to Leo. "Awesome!"

"It's not whipped cream," Merganzer said, leaning down closer to the boys and shaking the can with all his might. "It's something much better than that."

"Better lean back," the dapper man with the cane said. "This could get ugly."

But it was much too late for that, because Merganzer didn't have a can of whipped cream, he had a can of

Glooooob, the amazing, sour, sweet, syrupy, sparkling perfection that Dr. Flart had invented in his laboratory under the Whippet Hotel. The canned kind was highly volatile, and once Merganzer started spraying, the stuff was flying out like foam from a fire extinguisher. Green fizzy glop flew up into the trees, slathered every person in the gathering, and covered most of the table before Merganzer finally tamed the can and directed its contents to Leo's and Remi's plates.

"I hate when he does this," a large man who looked more like a walrus than a person said. His very bushy mustache was covered in Glooooob.

"Eat fast!" Merganzer said when the deed was done. "It won't last long, as you already know."

Leo was laughing too hard to start eating, but Remi knew better. The most amazing thing about Glooooob was that you could make the most spectacular mess imaginable with it, and within a few seconds it would start to evaporate into thin air. By the time Leo looked down, the Glooooob on his plate was already beginning to evaporate. Remi slurped up everything but the pancake on his plate with a disgusting sucking sound that sent Leo and Merganzer into howls of laughter while everyone else sat silently watching, not the least bit amused.

"I suppose we should be getting on with it," Merganzer said, wiping a laughter-induced tear from the corner of his eye. The last of the Glooooob disappeared as Merganzer set the can on the table and looked suddenly serious. "It's time I told you all what's really going on here."

Remi, who could be very fast when he wanted to be, grabbed the can of Glooooob and pointed it into his mouth, firing until green fizz poured down his face.

"Leo, if you please," Merganzer said. Leo, being the slightly more mature of the two boys, took the can from Remi.

"All is about to be revealed," Merganzer said, cracking one more hiccup of a laugh before he, too, was ready to proceed.

"You have all been running hotels owned by me for some time now," he began, and everyone at the table either gasped or looked quizzically at him. "That's right. Through a complex collection of holding companies, I own all of the hotels you represent. I'm sure Blop or Mr. Powell could explain it to you, but really — none of those details matter. The only thing that *does* matter is that we are about to begin a competition that will forever alter your lives."

"Say, what's this all about?" The man with the very long face and the even longer pointed beard was reaching the limit of his patience. "And why did the top of my hotel end up here? And, while we're at it, where *is* here?"

"I'll get to all those details right away, I promise. But first let me introduce you to one another. You're going to want to know who you'll be competing against."

"Competing for what?" the large man who looked like a walrus asked. He was sitting directly to the right of Merganzer.

"Everyone, this is E. J. Bosco," Merganzer said, ignoring the walrus man's question as he introduced him. "Bosco runs the Boomtown Hotel on the Lower East Side. Lively place, lots of parties. The top floor of the Boomtown Hotel is sitting over there, thataway. I've taken the liberty of collecting all the roofs of all my hotels and bringing them here."

"Why, that's insane," said the very tan woman, who was sitting next to E. J. Bosco. "You can't just remove the tops of hotels. It's not done!"

Merganzer leaned forward, placing the tips of his long fingers on the table.

"Well, of course I can. I just did."

"Yes, but —"

"Miss Harrington, if you please," Merganzer said. "The Rochester is a fine hotel, even without its top."

Leo was beginning to understand. For whatever reason, Merganzer had built a lot of hotels and created them so that, when he was ready, he could remove the tops. Leo had a pretty good feeling that Merganzer was actually *hiding* all those roofs as he got them ready for some mysterious reason. This was getting exciting.

Merganzer next introduced the man with the long face and beard.

"This is Mr. Pilf, who runs the Spiff Hotel."

"*You* run the Spiff?" asked E. J. Bosco. The two men came from completely different worlds, but Bosco clearly respected Mr. Pilf from the start. "That's a very fine hotel, I must say."

"Why, thank you," Mr. Pilf said, though he had nearly nothing to do with whether the hotel was very fine. He, and the others, *ran* the hotels. It was Merganzer who had built them.

"Miss Sheezley runs the Foxtrot Hotel on Long Island," Merganzer continued. "We had to do a lot of work in the middle of the night on that one. Very curious people, Long Islanders."

"You're pretty curious yourself, Whippet," Miss Sheezley snorted. She was wearing lots of makeup and had large eyes that were constantly wide open with surprise. They were eyes that looked like they could swallow up all of outer space.

"And last, Mr. Alfred Whitney, of the Paddington Hotel in Westchester," Merganzer said, acknowledging the dapper, cane-bearing man who looked like an aristocrat.

There was an uncomfortable silence at the table as everyone realized Merganzer had neglected to introduce Leo and Remi.

"Are these your children?" Miss Sheezley asked. There was a certain something in her voice that Leo and Remi understood immediately: Miss Sheezley did *not* like children.

"Oh dear, I've completely forgotten Leo Fillmore," Merganzer said, laughing nervously as he looked down at the two boys. "Leo runs the Whippet Hotel, which I suppose I should mention is my very favorite hotel of them all."

A murmur of displeasure moved across the table. Everyone wanted *their* hotel to be Merganzer's favorite. But they also knew about the Whippet. There were thousands of hotels in New York — they were opening and closing all the time — so none of them could be expected to know about every hotel. But *everyone* knew about the Whippet. It was famously weird, outrageously exclusive. The fact that a kid was running it was a double insult.

"Why on earth would you have a child running a hotel?" Mr. Pilf said the words like he was spitting them out of his mouth. He was not an attractive talker.

Merganzer ignored the question and moved on.

"Leo has brought with him his newly minted stepbrother, Remi. These two are a very resourceful pair, I warn you."

"And I brought a robot," Remi said, though he didn't take Blop out of his pocket and show him around. If this really was a competition, Blop could be a secret weapon, with his vast knowledge of the Whippet Empire.

"Come along then, we're walking," Merganzer said without any warning at all. He was up, taking off the apron and the tall white cooking hat, before any of the guests could question him further about why he'd put a child in charge of arguably the most famous hotel in the world.

"If I were running the Whippet, it would be making money. Lots of it," Bosco said under his breath.

Leo heard the remark but held his tongue. Inside he was feeling, for the first time in his life, a sense of competition about his work. Running a profitable hotel had never occurred to him. He'd only ever wanted to keep the Whippet running in tip-top condition. Profit was a new idea, one he wasn't sure he liked very much.

As Merganzer walked, he began to explain what was going on. Falling behind might mean missing an important detail, so Leo grabbed Remi by his red jacket and pulled him away from the can of Glooooob before Remi could reach for it.

"You are standing in a very secret place: the field of wacky inventions. It was left to me by my father many years ago, and it sits on the most precious undeveloped parcel of land in the whole of New York State. The land is three square miles in size, but I only use what's inside the walls — that amounts to approximately five football fields, give or take a yard."

Merganzer snaked through the trees, walking quickly as everyone tried to keep up, hanging on every word.

"The large tent to your right is for you to explore, should you feel there might be something worth finding inside. I really can't say what's in there. Stuff. Lots of stuff. The building far off over there is by invitation only. It's for your own good, because of the tests going on inside."

"What kinds of tests?" Leo asked, hoping but not expecting an answer.

"We're using the Wyro in there, trying to fire something big. Big, big, big."

Leo knew about the Wyro, because he was the one who had retrieved it from under the Whippet Hotel. It was small, like the size of two yo-yos glued together, and it was extremely powerful.

"What's a Wyro?" Miss Harrington asked curiously.

"Never mind that, just don't go in the building and start searching around. There are some things that go bump in the night, and you definitely do not want to run into any of those. And Lucy, a twelve-foot chicken. She's excitable. Here we have the electric eel ponds — very useful sources of energy, but don't get too close."

Leo looked at the four small ponds and noticed little bolts of electricity traveling between them. There was also a long extension cord hanging down from a tree, the end of which was hidden in the blue-green water.

"What's the cord for?" asked Miss Sheezley.

"Oh, that," Merganzer said, continuing on past the ponds. "That was for heating the pancake griddle."

Merganzer pulled a key card out of his jacket pocket and tried to hide the fact that he was whispering something to someone, but Leo heard.

"Unplug griddle, pronto. It's probably starting to overheat."

"Check," a small voice came back. "Unplugging griddle."

Leo wondered who it was, but there was no time for that. Merganzer was already talking again.

"Leo and Remi have seen inside the top floor of the Whippet. It's my private library, and I'm very happy to have it here on the grounds at last. It will no longer be the top of a hotel but, instead, the foundation of my very own *private* hotel. The rest of the floors will be made from the roofs each of you brought with you to the field of wacky inventions."

"But they're all scattered around," said the dapper Mr. Whitney. "That's not a hotel at all. It's just a bunch of hotel floors sitting in a field. And also, I've never been inside the top floor of the Paddington Hotel. It's not possible to get in there."

Everyone began to complain about the same problem. The top floors of all the hotels had always been secret floors, floors that could not be entered. None of the floors had windows, only ladders leading to the roof.

"You all climbed to the roofs of your respective hotels last night for a reason. I wanted you here, with me, so that we could unlock them together. Some of my greatest inventions reside inside these structures, and the time has come to put them all together."

Merganzer turned and faced everyone. "We must stack these floors and make a new hotel!"

"You, Merganzer D. Whippet, are off your rocker," Mr. Pilf said. "This entire operation is outrageous!"

"I'm inclined to agree," E. J. Bosco added. "No one told me I was going to be kidnapped and forced into a dangerous competition when I took the job. I'm a hotel manager, not a superhero."

"I know a superhero," Remi said. "Captain Rickenbacker. He's got a cape."

"Who asked you?!" Bosco screamed, and being the size and shape of a gigantic walrus, it scared Remi a little bit.

"Please don't yell at the children," Merganzer said sternly. "We'll have none of that, and I won't be giving any more instructions. I'll be making myself scarce, because I have big, big things to work on. But for those of you who think this is a fool's errand, know this: Whoever gets to the top of this hotel first will run *all* my hotels. I'm expanding into Europe. And Japan. The Ukraine is *very* promising. Someone needs to run the Whippet Empire here at home, and that someone is going to be one of you."

Now everyone — Mr. Pilf, Alfred Whitney, Miss Sheezley, and Miss Harrington — was singing a new tune. Even to the grumpy walrus-man E. J. Bosco, the idea of running an empire of hotels strewn across all of New York City was too enticing for words. It would almost surely mean a huge pay raise, stock options, and a seat at the pinnacle of the travel industry in America's most important city. It was, as Merganzer was fond of saying, big — very big indeed!

But Leo and Remi were thinking of something altogether different. They couldn't have cared less about owning or running more hotels. All they could think about as they looked around the field of wacky inventions was what lay hidden inside each floor and how much fun it would be to stack them one on top of the next.

"Is this the part where you say *the game is afoot*?" Mr. Whitney asked with a sly smile. Leo and Remi liked this Alfred Whitney character. He was like Sherlock Holmes and he had an excellent, slow voice that was deep and commanding.

"I believe you're right, Mr. Whitney," Merganzer said. And with that, he turned and wandered off in search of ducks or electric eels or twelve-foot chickens, calling over his shoulder: "The game *is* afoot! May the best man, woman, or child win!"

• CHAPTER 5 •

THE SECOND FLOOR GOES UP

Most of the hotel managers stared awkwardly at one another as Leo and Remi finished their pancakes back inside. It was one thing to have a hotel empire within your reach, another to know how to get one's hands on the prize. No one seated at the table had ever been asked to build a hotel, and certainly not in the weird way that Merganzer was asking them to do it. No one, that is, except Leo and Remi. They'd already been on two such adventures — one inside the Whippet Hotel and one underground, beneath the very same building.

"Has anyone else been inside the top floor of your hotel?" E. J. Bosco asked. He was raring to go, but he had no idea where to start.

Remi began to say yes, of course, he'd been in the Whippet Hotel library lots of times. But Leo felt it was a piece of information best kept secret. He elbowed Remi in the side, but Mr. Pilf with the long face and the longer beard took notice — he could tell Leo and Remi knew something he did not.

Miss Sheezley's huge eyes grew even larger as her eyebrows raised, and she started whispering something to E. J. Bosco. A second later, both of them were up out of their chairs, hastily walking away. They made an odd pair, a walrus and a bug-eyed woman, but clearly they'd struck up some sort of bargain. This seemed to get all the other hotel managers nervous, as if they should be putting together alliances of their own.

"Shall we make a go of it together, at least for a while?" Miss Harrington asked the dapper Alfred Whitney. They were perfect for each other, like two people pulled out of a black-and-white movie, and Leo expected Alfred to say yes.

"I'm afraid I'd only hold you back," Alfred said, lifting his cane ever so slightly. "I'm a little slow on my feet. Football knees."

"You played football?" Remi asked.

"At the University of Oregon," Alfred said proudly, tapping the golden duck on the end of his cane. "I'm a Duck, through and through. Also a running back."

While this small conversation took place, Miss Harrington looked Mr. Pilf up and down. He was the most annoying person in the bunch unless she wanted to partner with two kids or an old man who would surely slow her down. She turned her gaze on Remi, thinking.

"Don't look at me," Remi said, putting an arm around Leo. "I've already got a partner, and I'm not trading."

Miss Harrington was in mortal danger of going it alone, an unacceptable outcome at this stage of the game. She put all her charms into play, standing as she reached out her hand in Mr. Pilf's direction. He was not a man who had enjoyed very many dates (work was his girlfriend), and he was obviously smitten with Miss Harrington. He rose to his feet and the two of them moved away, plotting and scheming.

"Well, I'm feeling lucky," Remi said, standing as he stretched his arms toward the sky. "And full. Let's get this show on the road, partner."

Leo looked at Alfred, who he'd taken a real liking to. He had a thought just then, that this really was the man for the job. Leo had zero interest in running an empire of hotels, but he sure didn't want to end up with Mr. Pilf or E. J. Bosco as a boss. That spelled Disaster with a capital D. And so he said what he truly felt, which was something that only a kid would do at a time such as this.

"Mr. Whitney," he began.

"Oh, please, call me Alfred."

"Okay, Alfred. I'm not even twelve yet, but me and Remi here have had a couple of Merganzer D. Whippet–size adventures already, and I have to say, we really enjoy having them."

"That we do," Remi agreed. "Nothing like a Merganzer adventure! They're the best."

"And we kind of have our hands full running the Whippet Hotel. It's our home."

Remi could already tell where Leo was going, and he liked it very much.

"So what I'm thinking is this," Leo went on. "You seem like a very nice guy, the nicest of the bunch, and we don't really have any interest at all in running six hotels. We're happy taking care of just one."

"Helps that it's the best hotel in the world!" Remi added.

"What are you thinking?" Alfred Whitney asked, rising from his seat and slowly backing away from the stone table.

"What if we work together — the three of us — with the goal being that *you* end up winning?"

"That way we can enjoy this awesome adventure and not end up with more work when it's done!" Remi said, which was exactly what Leo was thinking.

Alfred looked at the two boys with great affection. He smiled wistfully, shaking his head back and forth a few times.

"These hotel managers would be quite a handful, wouldn't they?" he concluded.

Leo gazed off through the trees, where E. J. Bosco was giving him the evil eye.

"I believe you're right," Leo answered.

Alfred nodded then, with real determination, and put out his hand.

"I humbly submit to your plan. And furthermore, I promise to leave you fully in charge of the Whippet Hotel should we meet with success."

"For the record, Leo *owns* the Whippet," Remi said. "I'm not even sure why we're doing this."

"Fair enough," Alfred said. "I'll oversee the rest of Merganzer's hotels if we win and provide any help you need."

Leo looked at Remi and they nodded. Then both boys shook Alfred Whitney's hand.

"Let's get busy!" Remi declared. "We have a competition to win!"

The three of them — Leo, Remi, and Alfred — spoke at length on the maddeningly sluggish walk. Alfred really was slow on foot. They decided that the Whippet was indeed the foundation for the new hotel. Why else would it be the only one without an airship hovering overhead? The Whippet was where they were most likely to discover a clue about how to begin, and so it was there they ventured first.

It took them almost twenty minutes to walk back to the top floor of the Whippet Hotel, and another five minutes to scale the ladder that led to the roof. There they found Miss Harrington and Mr. Pilf examining the duck elevator.

"Oh, great," Leo said. "We've got company."

"How does this thing work?" Mr. Pilf yelled across the roof. "And where does it go?"

The door to the duck elevator was closed. Had it been open, they might have been able to ride the small elevator into the library below, but the only thing that would open it was the master key card in one of Leo's many pockets. Betty, the resident duck, and her string of six obedient ducklings waddled toward Leo and Remi in search of crackers.

"We should've brought her a pancake," Remi said.

"Oh, I might be of some assistance there," Alfred said, digging into his coat, which bore a strong resemblance to a tuxedo jacket.

"Is anyone hearing me?" Pilf yelled. "How does this thing work?"

Miss Harrington was sitting on a marble bench by the pond, looking as though she was thinking very deep thoughts. Alfred produced a green plastic package from his pocket.

"I always carry a few granola bars around, just in case I'm lost on a hike up Mount Everest."

Remi and Leo looked blankly at the cane. This guy wasn't hiking across the street, let alone up a mountain.

"That was a joke," Alfred said. "And here are the ducks."

Alfred opened the package and broke the first of two granola bars into pieces. The ducklings went mad for the treat, and Betty seemed happy for them.

Leo took a long look around, hoping to find a clue to what they were supposed to do. Mr. Pilf and Miss Harrington had both moved away from the duck elevator door. It appeared they had no patience for puzzling dilemmas. Leo could have opened the door with his Whippet Hotel key card if he'd wanted to, but he wasn't about to do that, not until he was sure they should even be going down into the library.

"Odd," Remi said. "The golden duck is gone."

Leo remembered the golden duck, where the zip rope had been carefully tied in place. It had been sitting on a golden pole in the middle of the pond. Remi was right! The golden duck *was* gone, or at least it had been moved.

"Oh, wait," Remi said, as if it didn't really matter. "It's right there."

He pointed to the far corner of the hotel roof, and sure enough, the golden duck was standing there, looking like it had never moved. As they walked toward it, the golden duck suddenly dropped out of view.

"Squirrelly duck," Remi said.

"It's a clue," Leo concluded with a whisper, putting his finger to his lips as he glanced over his head and watched Mr. Pilf turn their way, curious about what they were up to. Both he and Miss Harrington could smell a clue and began walking toward Leo, Remi, and Alfred. As soon as they did, the golden duck popped up behind them on their corner of the hotel roof. Remi almost spilled the beans, but Alfred poked him gently in the side with his cane, just in time.

"Oh, right," Remi whispered as their competitors neared. "It's a clue."

"You two distract them; I'm going in for a closer look," Leo said.

Leo rounded the pond in the middle of the roof, acting like he had no idea what he was really looking for, and soon arrived alone at the golden duck. He noticed right away that it was not the same one he'd tied the zip rope to. This duck didn't have a leg that moved when he pulled on it. Leo tried to twist the golden duck's head, but nothing happened. Then he pushed down on the tail and it moved. Out of the mouth of the golden duck came a strip of orange ticker tape.

"I've found a clue!" Leo whispered to himself, and just as he did, the golden duck swooshed down, out of sight, the orange strip of ticker tape breaking off in Leo's hand.

"What's going on over there?" Miss Harrington yelled, advancing on Leo rapidly, with Mr. Pilf close behind. Her black hair and his white beard made for a startling combination. Leo turned away from them and read the orange ticker tape. He only had a moment, but a moment was long enough! He took out his special, one-of-a-kind Whippet Hotel key card and pressed a few buttons. Then he turned around as if nothing very special was happening. The duck elevator door opened up — Leo had opened it — and Pilf jumped back as if he'd been hit in the face with a water balloon. There was quite a look of shock on his face, but he gamely covered it by stating the obvious.

"Aha! Look there, the door has opened!"

"You don't say," Miss Harrington said sarcastically. She had no patience for buffoons.

Betty, thinking that an open duck elevator was an invitation for a duck walk, waddled across the roof, with her ducklings tailing close behind. Comet, the smallest of them all, kept circling Alfred's feet, searching for more food.

"Well, well," Miss Harrington said as she came alongside Mr. Pilf at the door. "You're more useful than I thought you might be."

It was the worst kind of backhanded compliment, but Mr. Pilf melted under the warm attention he was getting from the former beauty queen. She took a long look at the small space as Betty passed by, as sure as any duck could be that she and her ducklings were bound for a walk around the grounds.

"Oh my, I've left my hat on the bench by the pond," Miss Harrington said to Mr. Pilf. "Be a dear and fetch it for me, won't you?"

She watched as Mr. Pilf, like a love-struck zombie, nodded and marched off toward the bench. Never mind that Miss Harrington hadn't been wearing a hat. She hated hats and never, ever wore them. She crouched down low and squatted in the elevator as Betty honked in her face and the ducklings climbed up and down her expensive leather shoes. It was all supremely unladylike, and by the look on her face she was not enjoying any of it. Still, she managed a smile as she pulled the lever, feeling, it seemed, quite sure she'd gotten the better of all the boys.

"Ta-ta," she said as the doors began to close. "I believe this round goes to yours truly, wouldn't you say?"

The doors closed all the way shut and Miss Harrington was gone, along with Betty and her ducklings, on their way into the Whippet Hotel library.

Mr. Pilf was crestfallen. For the briefest of moments he'd forgotten all about the possibility of owning an entire empire of hotels. He'd been bitten by the love bug, but how fleeting it had been. He slumped onto the bench and stared at the pond, despondently pulling at his long, thin beard.

Alfred Whitney didn't seem to have the heart to let him suffer so. Limping over with the help of his cane, he offered Pilf a granola bar from his tuxedo pocket.

"You know, it's a complicated game," Alfred said. "Not this silly competition. I mean this business with the ladies. They are *very* complicated. But I have to tell you, I saw a twinkle in her eye."

It was possibly a white lie, but a nice one, and for that reason alone excusable to Leo and Remi.

Mr. Pilf perked up, taking the granola bar in hand and biting into it with gusto.

"Maybe you're right."

"Well, of course I am," Alfred replied.

A sound, like the weight of something tremendously heavy being lifted into the air, drifted across the field of wacky inventions.

"I think this hotel is about to get a second floor," Leo said. He passed the orange note to Remi, who read it with great excitement. It was a Merganzer D. Whippet message, the kind Leo had become very good at figuring out.

> Open the door and send the duck.
> If _you_ go down you're out of luck.

"Nicely done, Leo," Remi said. "I'm not sure I would have figured it out that fast."

"I hope she'll be all right," Alfred said, looking at the duck elevator door, which remained closed. The fact that it was now moving down with Betty inside appeared to be the trigger that had set the next floor in motion.

"It's safer inside than it is out here," Leo said. He was looking overhead, where the floor of a hotel was descending toward them. There was very little time to get off the roof of the Whippet Hotel, and Mr. Pilf was rapidly losing his nerve. He was not good under pressure.

"We'll be crushed!" he yelled, tossing what was left of the granola bar over his head as he ran for the ladder.

It was then that Leo realized there was one little duckling that hadn't followed all the rest into the duck elevator.

"Guys, we have a duck problem," Leo said, trying to keep his cool as Mr. Pilf looked on from the edge of the hotel. Leo pointed at Comet, who was trying with all his might to swallow a chunk of granola bar bigger than his head.

"Comet!" Remi yelled. The duckling with the white racing stripe of fur down its back stared at the pond like he was getting ready to make a run for it.

"You go — I'll get the duckling," Mr. Whitney offered. But he was the slowest of them all, the least qualified to catch a lightning-fast duckling trying to get away with a treat.

Mr. Pilf, showing surprising mettle, ran back in the direction of the group, yelling for Alfred to get off the roof.

"You'll barely make it!" he said, looking up as the shadow of the building was cast over the Whippet

Hotel. It was only fifty feet overhead and descending fast.

But Mr. Pilf could not have been more wrong. Alfred Whitney was a Duck, through and through, and kneeling down he opened another package of granola bars, broke off a small piece, and called the duckling.

"Come here, Comet. Come on, little guy. You can do it."

He held out his hand, which was filled with crumbs. Comet was smart enough to realize the hunk he had ahold of was not going down his throat. He dropped it and started for Alfred's outstretched hand.

"Guys, I think there's a better way here," Leo said.

"No kidding!" Mr. Pilf yelled, looking up at the crushing weight of what was coming. "Like getting off the roof!"

And that was it for Mr. Pilf. He'd lost what little nerve he had, running to the ladder for good this time.

"No, I meant there's a way inside," Leo said, smiling broadly as Mr. Pilf vanished off the side of the building.

Leo pointed up, where a square space about the size of two refrigerators was notched out into the bottom of the building. It was a space big enough for three people, a tiny robot, and a duckling to stand in. Comet sat in

Alfred's hand, nibbling pieces of granola, while Remi looked up.

"I see it!" Remi shouted, grabbing Alfred by the coat. "Come on, this way!"

The second floor of Merganzer's hotel was only fifteen feet from landing on the Whippet Hotel roof as Alfred limped along, placing Comet in his pocket. Remi pulled Alfred as fast as he could go, until the building was so low they had to crawl the last few feet. A loud gnashing of hotel parts landing against other hotel parts filled the air around them as the second floor locked into place.

And then, as if all the lights in the whole world had gone out at once, everything went dark.

• CHAPTER 6 •

IN THE SHADOW OF A MONSTER

"Miss Harrington, are you in there?"

Merganzer's voice echoed through the Whippet Hotel library as if it were being broadcast through a long pipe. To Miss Harrington, who had been searching for clues and trying to avoid the ducks, it sounded like someone yelling into a canyon, a voice echoing off the tall shelves of books.

"Is that you, Mr. Whippet?" Miss Harrington called back, for truly she did not like being all alone in the empty library. The bookshelves towered all around her, and there had also been that business of all the noise overhead, as though a giant boulder had landed on the roof of the library.

"It is me!" Merganzer's voice reverberated though the library. "We'll need to get the ducks out at once. Also, you've been disqualified. I'm afraid you've managed to find yourself trapped under another floor. Very unfortunate."

"Am I really out of the competition already? How depressing!" Miss Harrington yelled as she made her way toward the sound of Merganzer's voice. The lights in the library flickered on and off, which got her to thinking the whole place might come crashing down around her. "Wasn't this the roof of the Whippet Hotel at one time?"

She had come to a hole in the side of the building that did not look big enough for her to crawl through. There was light on the other side, four feet down a tunnel, and also the black shadow of Merganzer's head. He had turned sideways, so she could see his silhouette in profile. The shadow of his long, crooked nose was on full display.

"It *was* the roof; that's correct!" Merganzer said, sounding very pleased with himself. "And now it's been returned to where it belongs, where it was before. It's a foundation again, as it should be. Don't you see?"

Miss Harrington pondered these words for a moment and realized she was almost certainly dealing with a genius and a madman. Betty flew up into the air and waddled down the tunnel toward Merganzer, while the ducklings struggled and failed to climb the wall. Miss Harrington took pity on them, picking them up one at a time and placing them in the round passageway. They waddled and fell over and waddled some more, and eventually all the fowl were clear of the library, standing outside where Merganzer fed them animal crackers.

"How do I get out?" Miss Harrington asked. She was not fond of ducks, but now that they were gone and she was alone, the bookshelves bothered her even more. And she felt something else, an emotion she knew all too well and tried very hard to avoid: loneliness. She heard a loud noise overhead and felt the ground shake under her feet.

"Settling in, that's all," Merganzer said, although his voice cracked like he wasn't so sure of himself. "I hadn't really planned to have someone in here just yet. Maybe you could read a book. I'll send food."

"You don't mean to leave me in here!" Miss Harrington was becoming just a little bit hysterical. "There must be a door. Or that small elevator — what about that?"

Merganzer shook his head. "No, that's not going to work. And there are no doors, not yet."

"Well, make one, you imbecile!"

Miss Harrington had forgotten that Merganzer D. Whippet was her boss and quite possibly the only person who could get her out of the predicament she was in.

"I'll send in some tea, pronto!" Merganzer said. And then he was gone, for he hated confrontations, and besides, he wanted to play with the ducks, not talk to a hotel manager.

"Merganzer!" Miss Harrington yelled. But it was no use.

Merganzer D. Whippet was no longer there.

Leo, Remi, and Alfred were sealed inside four walls and a top made of frosted glass, the kind that can't be seen through. They could make out shapes in the distance, and movements and strange sounds, but they could not see into the vast room beyond the glass, where the second floor of the new Whippet Hotel lay hidden. There were things moving out there, but they couldn't see what they were. Black letters in all different shapes and sizes were trapped inside the glass. They looked fuzzy, like deep shadows, and they begged to be touched. So of course Remi touched one.

"I think I broke it," Remi said, because when he touched a letter *A*, it burst into gray like a pile of ashes under a tennis shoe. A second later, the letter *A* appeared inside the glass in a new place.

"Hmmmmm," Remi said, rubbing his chin. The situation was taxing his brain in a way that made his head hurt a little bit. He reached out and touched about twenty letters in the space of two seconds, then did his best karate kick to one side and then another, knocking out four more letters in the blink of an eye.

"He's faster than he looks," Alfred said as the letters all returned in different places inside the dusty glass.

"Oh yeah," Leo said. "It runs in the family. We're all like ninjas."

"*Lightning* ninjas," Remi added, popping his knuckles as he looked around with a perplexed look on his face. The frosted glass walls hadn't burst into a million pieces at the sheer force of his awesomeness.

"Look here," Alfred said, pointing his cane up to the ceiling but not touching a letter *I*.

"Hey, it's a message!" Remi shouted. "Good going, Mr. Whitney. I can karate chop that cane of yours in two if you ever, you know, find yourself crawling around on the ground and need it shortened."

"I appreciate that, Remi. Really."

Remi nodded and the three of them looked at the message written over their heads. Alfred had the most perfect voice ever — low and smooth like an old black-and-white movie actor's — and he read the words so everyone could hear them: *"I have a little house in which I live all alone. It has no doors or windows, and if I want to go out I must break through a wall."*

"It's a very Merganzer kind of riddle," Remi observed.

"For sure," Leo added. "And a very Merganzer kind of trap."

"Let's see what Blop thinks." Remi pulled the coffee-cup-size robot out of his red jacket pocket.

"Hey, Blop," Remi said. "Where would I live if I had a little house and I lived all alone and there were no doors or windows? Oh, and if I want out, I break down a wall."

Leo, Remi, and Alfred listened carefully as Blop, the tiny tin robot of many words, began deciphering the riddle.

"If there are no doors and no windows, then there must not be any glass. That rules out approximately ninety-three percent of all known structures in the category of 'house.' My calculations tell me . . . igloo."

"Yeah, but an igloo has a door," Leo pointed out.

"Not in the dead of night. Eskimos block the entry. It's a wall at night."

Alfred started punching letters in the frosty glass, first an *I*, then a G, and so on until he spelled out the word *igloo*.

Nothing happened.

"Got any other ideas?" Remi asked Blop, which was probably a mistake, because Blop always had many ideas on every subject. As he yammered on and on about Frank Lloyd Wright and Frank Gehry and their uses of doors and windows, Comet, who had been asleep in Alfred's jacket pocket, popped his head out and looked around. He made a squeaky duckling sound and shook his head awake.

"I've got it!" Leo said. "And it *is* a very Merganzer kind of riddle."

"Do tell," Alfred Whitney said, taking Comet out of his pocket and holding him fondly. The two were growing closer by the minute.

Leo started moving around the glass enclosure, searching for letters. As he did, Remi watched a shadow moving across the glass where no one else was looking.

Something was out there.

It was huge, like a monster.

And it was staring at them.

"Hey, Leo," Remi stammered as Leo began touching letters, first an *E*, then a G.

"It's an egg!" Leo yelled, looking up and reading the message once more. "'I have a little house in which I live all alone. It has no doors or windows, and if I want to go out I must break through a wall.'"

"I'm not so sure we want out of this thing," Remi said. He put Blop in his pocket for safekeeping and watched as the shadow came nearer. The shadow was so big it covered the whole back wall of glass and crept over the glass ceiling.

"There!" Leo said, "Another G, up high!"

Alfred lifted his cane and poked the G — spelling out *egg* — just as Remi screamed, "Don't do it!"

But of course it was too late. As soon as Alfred touched the G and spelled the answer to the riddle, the glass ceiling evaporated into fog. The walls, too. And through the wall of fog Alfred and Leo saw what Remi had seen — the shadow of a very large, unseen thing. Comet dove into Alfred's pocket and shivered quietly, as the one man among them pushed the two boys back and held his ground.

"Whatever it is, I'll protect you. Don't worry!"

It was the first time Remi or Leo had heard him take command, and it did make them feel a little bit better, even if the shadow was way bigger than Alfred was.

"Back, you beast!" Alfred said, waving his cane to and fro, cutting through the fog until the air cleared and the three of them saw the second floor of the new Whippet Hotel. The first thing they realized was that the beast they'd called out was only four inches tall. There was a bright light behind the little creature, which had made its shadow very big.

"Is that what I think it is?" Leo asked, walking out from behind Alfred. The two boys carefully moved forward, resting their elbows on the top edge of a squat glass wall.

"It totally is," Remi answered, his voice full of wonder. "It's a T. rex."

And it was. A miniature dinosaur was looking up at them, roaring with all its might, which sounded sort of like the electric shaver Captain Rickenbacker used to shave the hair off his knuckles (because, he said, hairy knuckles are for villains, not superheroes). The T. rex would have had a real fight on its hands against a hamster. It was *that* small.

"This is a tiny dino zoo," Remi said, looking around in every direction. "Coolest thing *ever*!"

Giant boulders and strange trees poked out along a path, creating all sorts of shadowy corners and secret places. Alfred and the boys spread out, walking past a lot more glass enclosures they could peer down into. They held the kinds of things that barely fit inside a boy's imagination.

"Check this out!" Leo yelled, and Remi came running, with Alfred limping behind. They all leaned over a low rail and looked down into a field filled with long-necked Brachiosauruses. Tail to head they were less than a foot long, but they still swayed in a way that made them look like they were moving in slow motion. There were six of them, and they were staring intently into holes in the floor, waiting for something to happen. A burst of green leaves appeared out of the holes and they began eating them contentedly.

"Hey — look at that!" Remi said. A span of glass and stone rose against a wall with flying creatures swooping back and forth through the air.

"Tiny Pterodactyls," Alfred said, for the prehistoric winged beasts weren't any bigger than hummingbirds. "Amazing."

They wandered around the miniature dinosaur zoo, marveling at new creatures around every corner, until they took a hard left around a rock and found two people they were hoping not to see.

Miss Sheezley and E. J. Bosco were standing in the middle of the path, staring back at them.

"Hello, boys," Bosco said, his broad, walrus face staring down at them as if they'd shown up at a private party where children were not allowed. Alfred was the first to notice they were acting as if they might be hiding something. He eyed them warily.

"It's all quite amazing, don't you think?" Alfred said as he took a step closer and Miss Sheezley raised her chin, pointing the end of her nose down at him as she held her ground. Her eyes, as usual, were wide and startling.

"That's one word for it, I suppose," she said. "Another would be *outrageous*."

"I'll give you that," Alfred said. "Amazing *and* outrageous."

They swapped stories, though it was anyone's guess if Sheezley and Bosco were telling the truth or not. Leo and Remi informed them that, as far as they knew, Miss Harrington and Mr. Pilf were either hopelessly behind or out of the competition all together.

"Fine by me," Bosco said. "Less opposition, easier victory. It's simple math."

He glared at the boys with his watery eyes and his fat face, as if they, too, would be liked much more when they were not standing between Bosco and a hotel empire.

"We were on the roof of this floor when it started moving," he continued. "It's from Miss Harrington's hotel, the Rochester. A shame she won't be able to see it with us."

He chuckled happily, gazing around the astounding second floor, clearly pleased that Miss Harrington had ruined her chances. "Craziest thing you ever saw. It rose up under the power of that blimp and landed right on top of the Whippet Library."

"Then a trap door opened and there was a ladder," Sheezley said, pointing to the far end of the room. "Over there."

"It's closed now," Bosco wrapped up. "We're trapped in here with a bunch of dinosaurs. Good thing they're small enough to fit under my boot."

Leo thought that sounded terrible, like Bosco would be perfectly fine with stepping on a tiny Brontosaurus. He liked Bosco less every time the man opened his mouth.

"How about you lads go check on the ladder and the door?" Bosco said. "We'll keep searching" — he paused, touching the flab beneath his chin, and pointed in another direction — "that way. Yes, over by the T. rexes."

Remi started to protest, but Alfred jumped in. "That sounds like a plan. Let's work together, find a way out. There must be another riddle around here someplace."

He looked at Leo cleverly, and Leo took the hint.

"Come on, Remi — let's go check out that ladder. I bet there's a swamp on the way."

"A swamp? Let's do this!"

"Good luck, boys," Miss Sheezley said with the fakest kindness imaginable. "We'll let you know if we find something of interest."

It felt like walking through a low-flung jungle as they turned to go, with big floppy leaves hanging down from every direction and rocks that were just the right size to jump over. They didn't go very far before Alfred stopped them and knelt down, which seemed to require some painful effort on his part.

"Those knees of yours are really shot, huh?" Remi commented.

"The football field takes as well as it gives, no doubt," Alfred responded with a smile. "Now listen up, boys. I have a strong suspicion those two are hiding something. Why don't we split up, keep an eye on them?"

"I like that idea," Leo said. "It might require some crawling, though. How about I follow them while you and Remi check out the ladder?"

"Good plan," Remi said, looking at Alfred as he rose to his feet with a wince of pain. "Leo is a very stealth guy. He sneaks with the best of them."

"Thanks, bro," Leo said. It was the kind of compliment between two boys that meant something.

Their plan in place, Remi was off like a rocket, searching for more enclosures he could stare down into on the way to the ladder. He was far more interested in seeing live dinosaurs he could hold in his hand than unlocking the next floor.

"Check it out!" Leo heard Remi shout as they moved farther apart. "Raptors!"

Raptors, Leo thought, and wanted to turn back. They were his favorite dinosaurs, but there was important stealth work to be done. He got down on his knees as he came to a corner on the path and began to crawl along the edge.

"I don't understand," he heard Miss Sheezley complain. "Why must there always be riddles? It's maddening."

"Now, now, Miss Sheezley," E. J. Bosco said quietly. "We must stay calm, cool, and collected."

"And work fast," she added. "Those boys and that meddling Alfred Whitney won't be gone long."

As if Bosco sensed trouble already returning, he walked directly toward Leo, sniffing the air like a hound dog. Leo barely had enough time to crawl away before Bosco's black boots came into view. He inched as deeply into the dark shadows as he could, hoping he wouldn't get caught trying to watch them.

"I have something," Miss Sheezley said. "Come quick!"

Bosco was gone in a flash, and Leo found himself with his back against a vast, cold boulder. A low canopy of wide leaves filled the space around him. Sheezley and Bosco were standing before some sort of puzzle, but Leo didn't dare try to intervene. He was small, they were big, and he was outnumbered.

"You see there," Leo heard Miss Sheezley say. "It's a strand of DNA."

"I believe you're right," Bosco said. "But what does it mean?"

Their voices went quiet, like they were whispering to each other, and Leo tried with all his might to hear what they were saying. It is in times such as these that a tap on the arm can be highly upsetting, and so it was when Leo felt something *tap-tap-tapping* on his elbow. He barely contained his own voice, nearly screaming, as he jumped back and ruffled the leaves all around him.

"What was that?" Miss Sheezley asked, the whites of her eyes shaped like two chicken eggs. But then Remi howled with laughter from somewhere on the other side of the room. He'd found some very small dinosaur droppings and thought it was hilarious.

"Don't be so jumpy," Bosco said, stroking his walrus mustache with a shaking hand. He was becoming annoyed with Miss Sheezley. "You're making *me* nervous. And I *hate* feeling nervous. It's a useless emotion."

While all this was going on, something quite unexpected was afoot under the cover of darkness, where Leo had just gotten the scare of his life. As it turned out, he was not alone under the broad green leaves of the tiny dino kingdom. Someone had tapped him on the shoulder, and whoever that someone was, they had vanished into a hole in the rock.

And that someone was whispering.

"Come inside, where we can talk without being heard."

Leo didn't know what to make of the mysterious whisper, but it was not a voice that sounded like it was attached to a big person, and this gave him some comfort. It was an unexpected situation, but it was perfectly normal for a Merganzer D. Whippet adventure, so he followed the voice into the darkness of the hole, listening as the sound from outside fell away into a distant murmur.

Inside wasn't completely dark. In fact, there was a candle flickering in the middle of the space. It put off enough light for Leo to see a small hammock hanging in one corner, a stack of three books, a cup and a plate and a fork, and the most incredible thing of all.

There, in a dark cave on a hidden floor filled with tiny dinosaurs, sat a girl.

• CHAPTER 7 •

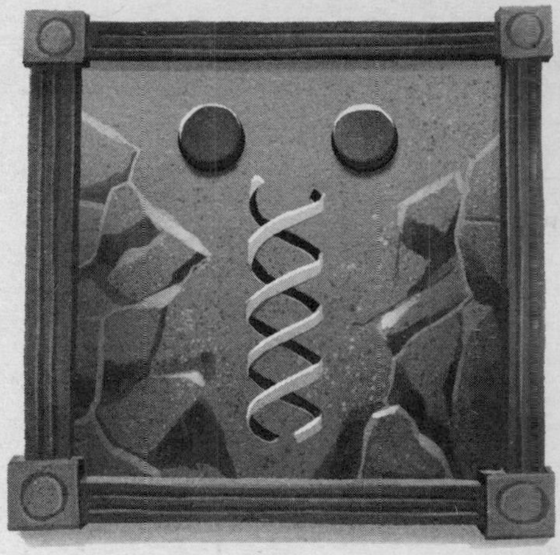

Lucy, Queen of the Dinosaurs

"How did you get inside?" she asked.

Leo didn't think the girl was angry; he thought she was confused, like she hadn't seen anyone in a long time.

"It's complicated," Leo said, because it was.

Leo observed her carefully and found that she was in many ways quite normal. She wore a pair of maintenance overalls like his own, and this intrigued him. She had bouncy hair with lots of curls and a face that looked bright and curious even in the shadows.

"I'd very much like to hear about why you're hiding in a cave," Leo said. "But right now, to be perfectly honest, I'm in the middle of something kind of important."

"So I gathered," the girl said, pulling her wildly overgrown hair into a loose ponytail and tying it off with a rubber band. "I think I can help you."

The girl dug inside of a pocket and pulled out a small T. rex, holding it in her hand like it was a precious stone. It roared a tiny roar.

"He only bites if he's trying to protect me," she said. "And I almost never need protecting."

"Good to know," Leo said. He could hear Miss Sheezley and E. J. Bosco arguing outside and felt his chances of staying in the competition slipping away with every second.

"I need to find out what they're looking at," Leo said. "It's a puzzle, or at least I think it is. It would be useful if I could figure out its meaning before they do."

"This is Phil," the girl said, looking at the T. rex. "And I'm Lucy."

"Phil?" Leo said, because it was a ridiculous name for a dinosaur, and they both knew it.

Lucy shrugged. "It seemed like a good idea at the time."

"Fair enough," Leo said, smiling, because the more he sat with it, the more he liked the idea of a T. rex named Phil.

"He's fast. Want to see?" Lucy asked.

"I do."

Lucy crept quietly through the hole that led to the cave and Leo followed her. He wanted to hear all about her story, but that would have to wait until there was less pressing business to take care of. Her ponytail flopped back and forth as she crawled away and then sat on her knees, gazing carefully out through the leaves. She looked back at Leo, and he realized she was even prettier than he'd been able to tell in the darkness of the cave.

"Don't worry about Phil," she said. "He can handle himself just fine."

"All right, I won't," Leo said, because after all, even if Phil was small like a gerbil, he was still a T. rex.

Lucy set Phil down and pointed him toward E. J. Bosco and Miss Sheezley. When Phil looked back at Lucy, she faked the most frightened face she could come up with. The little dinosaur looked at Bosco's pudgy ankle, narrowed his brow, and started marching away.

"I tell you it's DNA," Miss Sheezley said. "What else could it be? And what does it mean?"

"It must have something to do with all these dinosaurs. Whippet must have had access to dino DNA and figured out a way to make them small and harmless. One of them must be the key to unlocking the next floor."

Bosco heard a sound behind him that made him think of a bee buzzing in his ear. When he turned, Phil was standing in front of him, roaring as loudly as he could.

"Speaking of dinosaurs," he said. "We have a visitor."

"How perfect is that?" Miss Sheezley asked. "Here, take my scarf. You can catch him."

Bosco took the long scarf and wrapped it around his hand several times.

"There, now it can't bite me."

He advanced on Phil, but Phil was lightning fast. He darted to the left, jumped onto Bosco's boot, and scampered under his pant leg before Bosco knew what hit him.

Then Bosco screamed, because even tiny T. rex teeth sting when they chomp down on an ankle.

"It's trying to have me for breakfast!"

Bosco was slapping at his calf, yelling at Miss Sheezley to do something. She began kicking Bosco as hard as she could.

"Oh no," Leo said from his hiding place. "Will Phil be okay?"

Lucy looked quizzically at Leo. "He's a T. rex. You could hit him with a hammer and he'd just bounce right back up. Only he'd be angrier."

"Poor Bosco," Leo said as Miss Sheezley got in a particularly good kick, buckling Bosco to his knees.

"Yeah," Lucy agreed, shaking her head back and forth. "That is one sad dude."

Leo hardly knew Lucy, but he already liked her. She had a pet dinosaur. She was cute, and she dressed just like Leo. Leo concluded that Lucy was, quite possibly, the coolest girl ever.

Lucy's little dinosaur darted out of Bosco's pant leg and stared up at Miss Sheezley like she was a turkey sandwich. When Phil growled and took one step forward, she ran for her life, screaming about the insanity of it all.

"You don't scare me!" Bosco screamed at the top of his lungs. "Get ready to meet the bottom of Mr. Boot!"

Bosco lifted his leg and a shadow fell over Phil that must have felt to him like a solar eclipse. But Phil only narrowed his eyes even more than before, hopped back and forth on his hind legs, and waved Bosco in with his front claws.

"I feel sorry for him," Lucy said.

"Phil?"

"Heck no. That Bosco guy just sealed his doom."

E. J. Bosco's foot came down like an anvil, slamming into the pathway with startling force. Leo's breath caught in his throat, and for a moment he thought Lucy had been wrong about Phil. Had the little guy been smashed into a prehistoric pancake?

"T. rexes are super fast," Lucy assured him. "A lot of people don't know that, but it's true."

Phil reappeared just as she said this. He'd managed to climb up Bosco's back and perch on his shoulder like a parrot. And what was worse, Phil was staring at Bosco's floppy earlobe.

"Which way did he go?" Bosco asked out loud, although Miss Sheezley had long since arrived at the far end of the floor, searching for a way out. Phil appeared to be slowly digging the claws of his hind legs into Bosco's shoulder, and as Bosco turned in that direction, Phil bit down on his earlobe.

"That's *gotta* hurt," Lucy said as Bosco screamed. Phil started moving his head back and forth like a dog shaking a toy, and that's when Bosco started running. He had no idea where he was going, only that there was a searing pain in his ear the likes of which he had never felt before.

"He shouldn't go that way," Lucy said. "There's a hole over there."

"What do you mean, a hole?" Leo asked.

Just then he heard an echo-filled howling that sounded like someone was sliding down a tube, farther away with every passing second.

"Yup, he fell in," Lucy said. "Bummer. I was starting to really enjoy that."

"Well, don't be too bummed out," Leo said as he crawled forward and stood up on the path. "Bosco was kind of a meathead. I'm pretty sure one hotel is all Merganzer D. Whippet wants him running."

"I have no idea what you're talking about," Lucy said.

Before Leo could explain, Phil came running back all excited and bug-eyed. He was in a real lather.

"Calm down, Phil," Lucy said in a soothing voice. "You did a marvelous job protecting me. You're my hero."

She tossed him something that looked like a marble covered in mud. Phil gobbled it up in about two seconds flat.

"Dino treat," Lucy said. "It's kind of like dog food, I think. Wanna try one?"

Leo wished Remi was closer by. His stepbrother had been known to try fish food, cat food, monkey food, and bird food, just for the fun of it.

"No, thanks," Leo answered, wishing he were as daring as Remi when Lucy popped one in her mouth, chewed it like a Milk Dud, and put Phil back in one of her overall pockets.

"What now?" she asked.

"Now we try to solve a puzzle. Come on — you can help."

They walked the few steps required to arrive in front of the rock wall Miss Sheezley had been trying to hide, and the two of them took a good look. There was an image carved into the stone that did look a little bit like a strand of DNA — two lines twisted together so they resembled a barbershop pole. Above the marking were two buttons — one red, one blue.

"I found that first," a voice said from a ways off. Leo turned and saw Miss Sheezley standing on top of a boulder about twenty feet away, peering down through thick fauna. She wasn't about to come anywhere near Phil.

"Hey, Remi! Hey, Alfred!" Leo yelled as loud as he could. "Can you guys hear me?"

"Yeah!" Remi yelled back from about fifty feet in the opposite direction of Miss Sheezley. "But not very well. Yell louder."

"There's a puzzle here!" Lucy screamed — and, wow, she could really belt it out. Leo was pretty sure even Merganzer could hear her yelling from outside.

"You sound like a girl!" Remi said as he laughed. "Hilarious!"

Lucy looked at Leo curiously.

"Your friend sounds goofy," she said.

"He's my brother — well, stepbrother, but really my brother. He's a hoot. You'll like him."

"And Alfred has wandered off somewhere, looking for clues," Remi called out. "He's in here somewhere."

Lucy smiled and her button nose flattened out against her face. She turned her attention to the puzzle.

"I know how to solve this. It's not what you think."

Leo looked again at the symbol and the two colored strands. It did look like DNA, and he, like Bosco and Sheezley, assumed he'd find a dino enclosure with a creature that matched the DNA, along with some buttons to push. It wasn't much, but it was a start.

"Which dinosaur does this DNA match?" Leo said. "I bet that's where we should start. There must be some markings on the enclosures somewhere."

Lucy wasn't buying it. She had very different ideas about the puzzle.

"Would you mind terribly if I solved it for you? I've been wanting to do it for a while, but it takes two people and there's only one of me."

Leo felt suddenly sad for Lucy and wondered how long she'd been living on the floor and how she'd come to be there. And it was a complicated puzzle. He didn't think Lucy stood a chance of solving it, but he nodded anyway, just to encourage her.

Lucy stepped up to the puzzle and then turned in Remi's direction.

"Hey, kid!" Lucy screamed.

"His name is Remi," Leo offered.

"Who you calling kid?" Remi shot back. "And what's with the weird impersonations?"

"Are you all right over there?" Alfred Whitney yelled. He had returned to Remi's side only a moment before, hobbling in from the deep of the jungle.

"I'm fine! Just follow the instructions!" Leo yelled back.

"Whatever you say, Leo-patra," Remi cackled. He was getting a real kick out of Leo's voice talents, even if he had no idea why Leo was practicing them.

Lucy took charge, barking out instructions in rapid succession.

"If you push the vines away from the left side of the ladder, you'll see two buttons. Push only the red one."

There was a pause, then Alfred yelled back, "Done!"

Lucy turned to the puzzle and pushed the red button. A whirling sound emanated from behind the stone wall.

"Now the blue button! Push that one!" Lucy screamed.

"I tell you, that's my puzzle!" Miss Sheezley yelled. She had come down off the rock and was marching toward them with a new sense of purpose.

"Should we sic Phil on her?" Leo asked.

Lucy pushed the blue button. "Come on, run!"

"Wait, where are you going?" Leo asked, but he followed anyway, running in line behind her toward Remi and Alfred. He looked over his shoulder and saw Sheezley burst through the leaves onto the path, taking chase.

"Now grab the ladder by both sides!" Lucy cried. "And twist it as hard as you can. Don't stop twisting until it stops!"

Leo understood now — the puzzle image wasn't a DNA strand at all. It was the ladder that led down from the roof! Only it needed to be twisted in order to solve the puzzle, and the buttons needed to be pushed in tandem.

"Lucy, you're brilliant!" Leo said.

"That's nice of you to say," she said. "But hurry! I don't know how long it will stay open!"

Just then Leo felt a hand on the back of his maintenance overalls, jerking him to a stop. He wobbled back and forth, then felt Miss Sheezley push him off the trail into a thick pocket of prehistoric ferns. He was up in a flash, but one of his most prized maintenance tools had fallen out of his pockets — half a roll of duct tape — and it was rolling down the path in the wrong direction.

"It's opening up!" Leo heard Remi yell. "You gotta see this, bro! It's awesome!"

But Leo simply could not imagine his maintenance overalls without half a roll of duct tape resting in the wide leg pocket. It was like peanut butter without jelly: unacceptable.

And so he ran after it as it continued to roll away and took a sharp turn off the path.

At the ladder, Alfred was staring up into the ceiling.

"Mesmerizing, don't you think?" he asked Remi. "It looks like the ceiling is being dug out, but there's no dirt or debris."

And it did look that way. The ceiling was swirling away into a long hole over the top of the ladder. It looked like a milkshake in a blender, only upside down, and the hole kept getting longer.

"How come you're not climbing?!" Lucy yelled as she arrived at the twisted ladder.

"Who are *you*?" Remi asked, guarding the ladder like a chubby centurion.

"Can we talk about that later?" Lucy said. "There's a lady running after us and she kicks pretty hard."

When Lucy turned around, Miss Sheezley was standing there, out of breath and in a very bad mood. Her usually perfect poof of hair had gone crazy-fro on her head, and her lovely dress was crumpled and ripped. But that wasn't the really awful part. Miss Sheezley was doing something she never did. She was sweating.

"Disgusting," she said, swiping a bead of sweat off her brow. "Out of my way! All of you! I'm going up that ladder this instant!"

Lucy looked like she might take Phil out of her pocket and put him to work on Miss Sheezley, but she'd never seen an adult woman so angry. It was hard telling how a fight might go down between Phil and a sweaty wild woman who'd gone a little bit off her rocker.

"Be our guest," Alfred said, stepping to the side of the ladder and poking Remi in the shoulder with his cane. "Let the lady pass, Remi. We'll follow after. And really, it's only fair. She did find the puzzle first."

Remi's jaw dropped and his brow furrowed. "Leo's not going to like this. Not one bit."

Alfred lowered his voice and offered a warning to Remi: "We may find it useful not to be the first one up there."

Remi wasn't so sure. It never made sense in his playbook to give away a perfectly good lead in a race. Leads were hard to get, like rare comic books. When you got one, you kept it.

"Speaking of Leo, where is he?" Lucy asked, glancing

back in the direction from which she'd come. Miss Sheezley was already halfway up the twisty ladder before Lucy got her answer.

"Don't leave without me!" Leo yelled as he came into view. "I'm coming!"

"Ladies first," Alfred said, nodding gentlemanly at Lucy as she came near. "I've got a feeling you have a good story to tell. Am I right?"

"Pretty good," Lucy said, smiling at the enigmatic gentleman before her. She grabbed a ladder rung and started climbing. "See you at the top."

"That you shall," Alfred offered with another polite nod of his head.

Remi moved in close to Alfred and beckoned him near.

"Let me handle the interrogation with this new kid. I'm good at that stuff. She could be *really* dangerous. Like a master spy or something."

Alfred nodded, Leo arrived, and the rest of the party started climbing up the winding ladder. The ladder extended through the long hole, which they'd all arrived inside of, when the shadow of a head leaned over the opening at the top.

"Get out of my way — I'm coming back down!" Sheezley screamed.

And so it was that everyone on the long, twisting ladder climbed back down four or five rungs in order to make room for Miss Sheezley.

"The top floor of my very own hotel is out there," Miss Sheezley said, with characteristic awe in her voice. "It would have crushed me!"

But Leo and Remi only smiled. They'd made it through another portion of the contest, and they were still in it! And if this adventure was anything like all the others, the next stage would be even more dangerous and exciting than the last.

• CHAPTER 8 •

Lucy's Burp

A little while before Miss Sheezley found herself staring up at the roof of her hotel about to land on her head, someone else was making a very important call. It is not known for certain where or *who* this person was, only that he or she had found their way to a private place long enough to call Ms. Sparks and provide an update.

"Everything is going as planned. Miss Harrington is already out of the race!"

"Please tell me that's not all you've managed to rid us of. That Bosco character — now *he's* trouble. Have you gotten rid of him yet?"

There was a pause on the sat phone line.

"Working on it. He's a brute."

"And you are a fool!" Ms. Sparks roared. She was sitting in her crummy apartment, soaking her feet in a plastic kiddie pool she'd set in her living room. Water was splashing everywhere as she kicked her feet in frustration.

"Let me remind you — we are nothing with just one hotel. Nothing! Not if those boys or any of the other idiots end up running the whole empire. We could get thrown out on our cans! We must control *all* the hotels."

"I do understand. Really I do."

"I repeat: Do not lose track of Leo Fillmore or his intolerable sidekick, Remi. That boy couldn't open a door properly, let alone run an empire. But together they have Merganzer's favor. He's rigging this entire thing so they'll win! I know it!"

"That's not going to happen — I promise. I'm in control. I have them right where I want them."

"Stay on them! They're clever little urchins. They'll walk away with an empire and leave us with nothing if you're not careful."

"I better get back," the caller said. "I'll be missed. Don't worry — it's all going as planned."

"It better be."

Ms. Sparks hung up the phone and sloshed her long feet around in the shallow water of the kiddie pool. She began to smile, because for all her screaming and yelling, she was still in the hunt for the Whippet Hotel empire. She would rule from the shadows. *That lunatic Merganzer will never even know!* she thought, laughing to herself.

It was a diabolically brilliant plan . . . if only her accomplice could stay with those meddling boys.

E. J. Bosco was traveling exceptionally fast when he entered the Whippet Library for the first time. The tube he slid down turned in many directions on its path to the vast room of books below, and when it launched him out into the open air, he felt sure he'd eaten his last plate of chicken-fried steak (his favorite food, which was a specialty at the Boomtown, Bosco's hotel). He couldn't imagine living through a fall at that speed and from such a great height, but Merganzer D. Whippet was not a man who enjoyed seeing people expire inside any of his hotels, especially *this* hotel, which wasn't even finished yet. No, Bosco was not to die on that day, but he did find himself landing in a slightly painful and more-than-slightly ungentlemanly way.

Merganzer had rigged the exit from the tube so that the first thing a person would hit was a trampoline turned at a forty-five-degree angle from the floor of the library. The library was a tall space, forty feet or more, with tall shelves of books everywhere. Bosco belly flopped into the trampoline, landing on his legs, his chest, and his face. When it launched him back into the air, his limbs were flailing around so wildly that Miss Harrington, who was reading *20,000 Leagues Under the Sea* in a comfy chair down below, thought she'd seen an enormous flying octopus pass through her line of sight. (Stranger things than this have been seen in a Whippet hotel.) There were four more trampolines, also at forty-five-degree angles, that bounced E. J. Bosco ever closer to the floor as if he were a tennis ball bouncing down an escalator. He landed badly on the cold marble, but only his ego was bumped and bruised as he stood and took notice of his surroundings.

"Pull up a chair," Miss Harrington said as Bosco stumbled in her general direction. "I have a feeling we're going to be here until this ridiculous competition is over."

"Don't mind if I do," Bosco said, twisting as he cracked his back. "I've had about enough *competition* for one day."

The truth was, Bosco *hated* losing. They both did. But what were they to do?

"Times like these, it's hard to beat a good book," Harrington conceded. She picked the top volume off a pile of novels that sat beside her and handed it to her companion. Bosco sat down heavily, took the book, and kicked his feet up on a coffee table covered with a whimsical painting of a monkey riding an elephant.

"*The Wonderful Wizard of Oz*," Bosco said, and he smiled the way a walrus might smile, with a big, bushy mustache turned up on both ends. "You know, I've wanted to read this for quite some time. I'm rather glad I've been knocked out of these wacky proceedings. Does he send snacks?"

"Oh yes, every hour or so. We should be getting some tea and biscuits any time now."

"Marvelous!" Bosco said, and then he continued in his best British impression, "I do rather enjoy the tea and the crumpets. Delightful, don't you think?"

Miss Harrington was far too preoccupied with Captain Nemo's underwater adventure to pay any more attention to her new companion's attempt at humor. So E. J. Bosco took a deep, relaxing breath and turned to the first page of *The Wonderful Wizard of Oz*. Glancing momentarily up at him then, Miss Harrington understood how she had been feeling all afternoon. There was always time to work, never time enough to enjoy the pleasure of a good book. Being trapped in the Whippet Hotel library was a gift; it was what she and Bosco really needed — a small vacation with books to read and treats delivered by the hour.

More often than not, Merganzer D. Whippet knew what his managers needed even more than they did.

There were many well-documented incidents at Miss Sheezley's hotel, the Foxtrot, to earn her a reputation as a serious overreactor. Kicking E. J. Bosco with all her might was but one example of this aspect of her personality. Once, a single ant was seen crawling through her lobby, prompting a hotel-wide evacuation, followed by a room-to-room search-and-destroy mission for anything having the appearance of a bug. And so it was to be expected that Miss Sheezley's insistence on going back down the ladder was, probably, a little bit hasty.

"How long are we going to stand on this ladder?" Remi asked. He was getting tired of waiting around for Miss Sheezley to stop blocking their way out.

Leo had been able to glance around Miss Sheezley a little bit, and as far as he could tell, the top of her hotel wasn't anywhere near hitting bottom.

"I think maybe it's stopped," Leo offered. "Let's go out and have a look. We can't stay here all day."

Miss Sheezley reluctantly agreed to go back up — if only for a chance to get everyone out and then race back down the ladder to safety. She didn't like being in the pole position, where people were more likely to get hurt. Better to let someone else lead until the very end, then swoop in and take the victory.

When they'd all emerged into the light of day, Miss Sheezley stared up into the sky and had to admit she might have had one of her classic overreactions.

"It seemed closer than that," she said.

In fact, the roof of the Foxtrot Hotel, which was now being held aloft by an enormous blimp, was at least fifty feet overhead. And Leo was right: It looked as though it had stopped moving.

"It would appear that Merganzer isn't ready to continue just yet," Alfred observed. He glanced at his wristwatch, then began limping toward the middle of the roof.

"That thing could come crashing down at any moment!" Miss Sheezley said. "I say we stay close to the ladder in case we need to get out of the way in a hurry."

"Why not enjoy a bite of lunch instead?" Alfred countered. "After all, it's been laid out so nicely for us. Wouldn't you say?"

Leo had been too busy looking up at the building, which swayed slowly in the gentle breeze, to notice what Alfred had found.

"He's delivered some lunch, don't you see?" Alfred said as he arrived in the middle of the roof and looked back.

This got Remi's attention in a hurry, and Leo's, too. They hadn't eaten since breakfast, and they were both starving. Miss Sheezley's stomach growled, but she wasn't going anywhere near the lunch, because it was too far away from the ladder. She took two steps down and stood her ground, where she looked like someone standing knee-deep in a shallow pond. If the need arose, she would be the first one down the ladder to safety.

"Come on, Lucy, let's eat," Leo said, for he was sure the girl he'd found on the tiny dino floor hadn't eaten anything but dino treats for some time. "I know Merganzer D. Whippet. He wouldn't set us out a nice lunch unless he wanted us to eat it."

Lucy licked her lips, and it seemed to Leo that she was thinking of all the food she hadn't had in a long time. Her maintenance overalls — which he really wanted to know more about — looked about three sizes too big, like she'd shrunk since first putting them on.

"Race you," she said with a twinkle in her bright blue eyes, and before Leo could respond, she was running for the middle of the roof at a dead sprint. Leo took chase but found that Lucy was not only resourceful but also very fast. By the time he arrived at the picnic blanket, she was already sitting down. And Remi, never one to waste any time on formalities, was already chewing a mouthful of cheese and crackers. When it came to a race for lunch, Remi was faster than either one of them.

Merganzer had indeed provided a lovely scene on the former top of the Rochester Hotel. There was a large quilt with duck images sewn into it, plates of cheese and fruit, baskets of bread and crackers, and something else very special.

"Flart's Fizz!" Remi screamed. "No way!"

"What's Flart's Fizz?" Lucy asked, ripping off a piece of bread and handing it to Phil. The tiny dinosaur burrowed back out of sight in one of Lucy's many pockets and made a lot of munching sounds.

"What's Flart's Fizz?" Remi asked incredulously. "Only the best soda pop in the entire universe, that's all."

"Remi, be polite," Leo said. "How is she supposed to know what Flart's Fizz is?"

"I don't know what it is, either," Alfred said. He had arrived last, but wasted no time building a sandwich out of the bread and the cheese as Leo handed him a bottle. Remi gave bottles to everyone else, and found there was one left over.

"Hey, Miss Sheezley!" Remi yelled across the roof. "Wanna burp your brains out?"

"No, thank you," she replied tersely.

"Didn't think so." Remi smiled. Leo was pretty sure his brother was planning to drink the extra.

Remi popped the lid on his bottle and instructed everyone else to do the same as Leo explained about Dr. Flart, the incredible hidden underground floors of the Whippet Hotel, and the even more incredible burps that Flart's Fizz produced.

"Bottoms up," Remi said, tipping his bottle and guzzling all but the very last of its contents in one superhuman swig.

Alfred was game, drinking half of his bottle in no time flat, while Leo watched and waited. Remi's eyes went wide, like he was holding something gigantic inside that was getting bigger by the second. His mouth opened and he looked to the sky, letting rip a burp that started low and slow and built to a high-pitched wheezer of unbelievable awesomeness. About halfway through, Alfred chimed in with his own world-class effort, and the two performed a burping duet until, finally, after what seemed like a month, Remi's burp fizzled out. Albert quickly chugged the rest of his bottle and kept burping, like a big balloon slowly releasing air, until Miss Sheezley yelled, *"Disgusting!"* and he laughed and laughed. There's nothing quite like the sound of laughing and burping at the same time — in the pantheon of burpdom, this is known as lurping — and pretty soon Lucy and Leo were laughing, too. Then a magical sort of thing happened, a rare and wacky thing. From somewhere far below, there came a sound unlike any other — full of honks and whoops as it carried up through the trees.

"Merganzer!" Leo said, standing up and running to the edge of the roof in a flash. When he reached the rail and leaned over, he realized how far up into the trees they'd gotten. There were branches all around him, but there was a clear view to the ground where Merganzer D. Whippet could be seen walking the ducks.

"Merganzer!" Leo cried out. Merganzer stopped making his distinct laughing sound and looked up.

"Well, if it isn't Leo Fillmore! I thought I heard some burping. Or better yet, some lurping."

Remi leaned his head over next to Leo's.

"And Remi! Very glad to see you both safe and sound and still in the hunt."

“Thanks for the Flart’s Fizz!” Remi shouted. “That was a real pick-me-up.”

“How’s Betty doing?” Leo asked as Alfred hobbled near.

Merganzer looked down at the mother duck and her ducklings and shook his head.

“She’s in a bit of a funk. I can’t figure why. I’ve been giving her animal crackers and taking her for walks. But nothing seems to help.”

“I believe I know what’s bothering her,” Alfred Whitney said. He held Comet carefully in both hands, for Comet wasn’t a flyer just yet. He’d never make it to the bottom on his own. But he did make whatever that sound is that ducklings make, an almost honk.

Looking up, Betty went bonkers.

“I believe this is one of hers,” Alfred said. “That must be why she’s so upset.”

Merganzer D. Whippet looked thoughtfully at the duck in his charge and the duckling way overhead.

“Well, there’s nothing to be done just now. At least I know why Betty’s been so difficult.”

“And you know the first rule of an adventure,” Leo said.

Betty was honking like crazy, but Merganzer didn’t seem to mind.

"Always bring a duck!" Merganzer called out. "And Comet is a very good little duck." With a nod, he started off, his long walking stick before him, and the rest of Betty's ducklings followed.

"I enjoyed the burping," Alfred added. "First class."

Betty looked up. If it was possible for a duck to have a stern look on its face, this one did. It was hard to say if the last few quacks and the scowl were directed at Alfred (*you better bring my duckling back in one piece*) or Comet (*boy, are you ever gonna get it when you finally get down here*). Either way, she'd said her piece and at least knew her missing duckling was only on an adventure, not captured by a monkey or wandering off for a swim in an electric eel pond.

Lucy had stayed at the picnic all alone, staring at her bottle of Flart's Fizz. Leo felt sorry for her and became more curious than ever about her story.

"Let's show them what a *real* burp sounds like," Leo said, smiling at Lucy as he walked back toward her. Lucy smiled back nervously. She was not one to play it safe, and before Leo knew it, she downed her entire bottle of Flart's Fizz in five seconds flat, picked up the extra bottle, and downed that one, too.

"Whoa," Remi said, suddenly in awe of Lucy. He'd never seen a girl drink an entire bottle, let alone two bottles, of Flart's Fizz in one shot. Even he hadn't thought of trying that!

Remi and Albert made their way over to the picnic again as Leo tipped his bottle back and started gulping as fast as he could, hoping he'd be able to match whatever Lucy was about to produce.

Lucy's burp was, in a word, outstanding. Years later it would take on legendary status as one of the three biggest burps of all time. It was so big it nearly knocked Lucy off her feet. And it went on for twice as long as Remi's had. It had a long, deep middle that went on for half a minute, followed by a perfectly executed whiz-tail ending that left her with a beaming smile on her face.

"That was one incredible burp," Remi said. "No, seriously. Epic."

It was made even more so by the fact that Leo had drank a dud. Leo could muster only the most anemic of burps, a true runt in comparison to Lucy's masterpiece.

Phil was curious about all the noise, and when he stuck his head out, Lucy poured the last few drops of Flart's Fizz from her bottle down the dinosaur's gullet. There are few things in the world more hilarious than a salt-shaker-size dinosaur burping for a really long time.

It sounded like a miniature buzz plane sputtering through the air.

"I think he enjoyed that," Remi said when Phil was through. "I know I did."

There was, however, an awkward silence settling over the picnic as everyone but Alfred sat back down.

"If I get that close to the floor again this soon, it will take some work putting me back on my feet. I'll stand, thank you."

Remi looked directly at Lucy, and minced no words.

"Are you a spy, sent by our enemies to steal our secrets?"

"Remi, come on," Leo said, laughing nervously. "You're being paranoid."

"Then answer me this," he went on, taking Blop out of his jacket pocket and setting him in front of Lucy so he could help with the interrogation. "How come she's got overalls, just like you? And a tiny dinosaur in her pocket? *And* she burps like a county-fair champion! The only thing that could make her more appealing is if she were a ninja robot!"

Blop took this as a compliment and said as much. Remi had made a pretty good point: If Lucy were a spy, she'd attack at their weaknesses with her overalls, dinosaur, and championship burping.

"You guys are weird," she concluded, taking Phil out of her pocket and standing him in front of the cracker bowl. Blop was less alarmed than curious.

"*Tyrannosaurus rex*," he said. "Making one this small would require both DNA and an unrivaled knowledge of nanotechnology. Also microbiology."

Blop began to ramble, as was his habit, while Phil attacked the crackers. Lucy took a deep breath and told everyone assembled the truth of the matter.

"I used to live two blocks down and one block over from the Rochester Hotel in an apartment building."

She stopped there, not exactly sure how to proceed.

"You mean the hotel owned by Miss Harrington?" Alfred asked. Comet peeked out of his hiding spot in Alfred's jacket and saw Phil. Comet tried to fly out of Alfred's pocket, flopping and spinning, and landed badly next to the plate of crackers.

"Do dinosaurs and ducks get along?" Leo asked.

"I think dinosaurs *eat* ducks," Remi said. "Or they would have if there had been ducks, you know, a bunch of millions of years ago."

Phil stopped eating and turned his head to the side, like he wasn't quite sure what to make of Comet. The duckling was bigger than Phil, but not by too much.

Comet righted himself with some effort, shook his head very fast, and stood toe-to-toe with a T. rex.

Then he quacked.

Phil looked at Lucy as if to say, *What kind of wacky creature is this thing? Will it try to eat me?*

"Go on and play," Lucy said. "He's harmless."

Phil was very pleased with this answer, and the two small creatures began yapping at each other, as if they were carrying on a conversation. Then they both stood in the middle of the cracker plate and started eating.

"Okay, that didn't go as expected," Remi said. Blop rolled over next to them and began to explain the difference between birds and dinosaurs. Disaster averted, Lucy went on with her story.

"Anyway, the Cranstons, who run the crummy apartment building, are lazy. They watch a lot of TV. They took me in only because my previous foster home said I had a reputation for being handy. Which is true. I'm handy. Also, I'm a ninja."

"No way!" Remi said.

Lucy smiled, hiccupped, and burped in the space of one second.

"No, not really. But I do have ninja pajama pants."

"Cool," Remi said, nodding his approval.

"But where are your parents?" Leo asked.

"That's just it," Lucy said. "I don't have parents. At least I don't think I do. I've been in the New York City foster care system forever and ever. I've bounced around a little bit."

"And how did you come to find yourself inside a secret floor at a Whippet hotel?" Alfred asked.

"I guess I'm what you might call a stowaway," Lucy admitted sheepishly. "Sometimes, when there were things that needed fixing at the Rochester, the Cranstons would hire me out. Because I'm really handy."

"So you've said," Remi commented. He still thought she might be a spy, but even he was softening.

"It was kind of miserable, living in the basement with the Cranstons, but I loved the Rochester."

"I live in the basement of my hotel, too," Leo said. "And I do maintenance work. With my dad. Ever fixed an air-conditioning unit?"

"Sure I have. Lots of times."

Leo beamed. Remi never wanted to talk about fixing hotel stuff, but Leo loved this part of his life. He could have sat there and talked with Lucy about boilers, pipes, wiring, and old doorknobs for hours.

"Let's get back on track here," Remi said. "How did you end up inside that crazy dinosaur floor?"

"Well, I was fixing the elevator, which kept getting stuck between floor number seven and floor number eight. There were some wiring problems, that was for sure. And while I was digging around on top of the elevator, I looked up. There was an extra door, way at the top, that didn't belong."

"So you climbed up and found a secret entrance?" Alfred asked. He was more than a little impressed with her resourcefulness.

"Pretty much, yeah. The only problem was that once I got in I couldn't get back out. The door shut behind me and I could never get it back open. That was two months ago."

"Two months!" Remi said. "What did you eat?"

Lucy shoved a hand in her pocket and pulled out a handful of dino treats, which looked quite a bit like Whoppers. Remi grabbed two and tossed them in his mouth, crunching them into little bits.

"Tastes like dog food."

"I think so, too," Lucy said, tossing a couple in her own mouth and smiling as she chomped.

"You two are totally gross," Leo said.

"And then yesterday the floor began to move," Lucy continued. "I didn't know what to think. After that, you all showed up. And here I am. That's all there is to tell."

"That, young lady, is a remarkable story," Alfred said. "I wonder if the Cranstons are worried about you."

"I highly doubt that. And I don't think they'd let me keep Phil."

Lucy scratched under Phil's long neck, and the little guy made a sort of gurgling sound.

"He purrs like a cat," Remi said. "Nice."

"I know, right?" Lucy agreed, glancing back at the ladder leading down into the tiny dino floor. "I'd rather stay down there with Phil than go back and live with the Cranstons."

"I don't think it's going to come to that," Alfred encouraged her. "But you're in the middle of a competition you can't win. I'm afraid it's rather exclusive."

"Yeah," Leo said. "You have to manage a hotel to get in."

"Whoa," Lucy said. "That *is* exclusive. What if I just tag along? I bet I could be useful."

"We believe you," Leo agreed. "And I don't see the harm in it as long as no one else does."

"We can use all the help we can get," Remi chimed in. "And we can't break up Blop, Comet, and Phil. They're like a team now. Let's do this thing."

Albert thought about it. He was the adult among them, and everyone looked at him for confirmation.

"I suppose I could arrange to have you dismissed back into the foster care system. In any case, the Cranstons need to be told. I'll see that it's taken care of just as soon as our little adventure is over."

"Cool!" Remi said. He'd been completely bowled over by Lucy. "Three musketeers!"

"Make that four," Alfred said.

"I'm coming over!" Miss Sheezley yelled from the ladder where she stood. She'd been quiet for a while, but all this secretive talk had finally made her curious enough to walk out under the building hovering overhead. Before she reached the picnic, a voice carried across the roof.

"Hello, everyone — how are we doing?"

It was Mr. Pilf, who hadn't been seen since he'd taken a ladder down the side of the library. He'd gained a hat in his absence, a floppy sort of number that made him look like a Frenchman with his long, thin beard.

"What do *you* want?" Miss Sheezley asked, arriving at the blanket and snatching up a stack of little sandwiches Alfred had carefully put together. "I thought you were out of the competition."

"No, no — not out," Mr. Pilf said as his feet landed on the roof and he began walking toward them. He peered up at the building nervously, watching it sway slowly back and forth like a piano about to drop on his head. Lucy picked up Phil and hid him in a pocket before Pilf could see him.

"Who's this?" he asked as he arrived at the picnic. He was staring at Lucy, but it was Leo who answered.

"That's a friend of Merganzer's — Lucy is her name. She's along to help us. And she's handy."

"Unexpected," Mr. Pilf concluded, though he was more concerned with being let back into the competition than the unforeseen addition of another child in the mix.

Just as Mr. Pilf said this, and before Miss Sheezley could protest his entry back into the game, the floor above them began to move down.

"Look there," Alfred said, pointing his cane skyward. "I think the picnic is over."

A moment later the floor overhead wasn't just moving, it was *dropping.*

"To the ladder!" Miss Sheezley yelled, throwing her sandwiches over her head. Had she been a linebacker she would almost certainly have blocked anyone else racing toward the ladder so that she could get there first, but as it was, no one else was making a run for it. "Come on, you fools! You'll be crushed!"

"Are you seeing what I'm seeing?" Leo asked the remaining group.

Even Pilf could see the way in, and he nodded with all the rest.

"Look up, Miss Sheezley!" Pilf yelled, but he didn't have to. A way into the falling floor of Miss Sheezley's Foxtrot Hotel appeared before her.

"Looks like six spots," Leo said. "Let's spread out."

Six egg-shaped holes had opened up on the white bottom of the hotel floor above, and out of each egg-shaped hole, a beam of light shot down onto the roof where they stood. Six spotlights, six places to stand, and six people who could take up positions under each. Miss Sheezley ran right past the one she'd arrived nearest to and started down the ladder. She watched as all the other people on the roof spread out and stood under different spots.

"I don't like it," Miss Sheezley yelled, her eyes wide with terror. "I don't like it one bit!"

"Say hello to the Brontosauruses for me," Lucy said, smiling with excitement as she looked up into a hole only twenty feet above. The light coming out of the hole was so bright she couldn't see past it, but if the floor above was anything like the floor below, she was all in.

Miss Sheezley glanced down the twisted ladder and thought about what the rest of her afternoon might include. She would be alone in a tiny dinosaur zoo, eating dog food, not knowing when or if she'd ever be found and rescued. Or she could stand on the roof and be swallowed up by an egg-shaped hole, which would at least give her a chance of overseeing an entire empire of hotels.

"Oh, bother," she said to herself as her chance to decide neared its end. The roof of her beloved Foxtrot Hotel was only ten feet from landing. It was now or never.

"Come on, Miss Sheezley!" Leo yelled from the far side of the roof, where he stood under a beam of light. "Don't you want to know what's been on top of your hotel all these years?"

She did want to know, that was true, and maybe that alone was what finally made her decide to step out under the light and take her chances with what lay above, not below.

She stood as tall and thin as the egg-shaped hole arrived only a foot over her head. The hole wasn't big enough for two people, it was made for one person. She looked across the flat roof and saw Remi jumping up and down, reaching for the hole like the playful child she imagined him to be. Leo was looking at Lucy, as if he worried she might not be okay. Lucy was staring up into the hole with a look of wonder on her face. Alfred Whitney kept looking pensively between the children, like he was afraid for their safety. And Pilf — well, Mr. Pilf was not one to revel in exciting opportunities that came his way. He had his hands clasped over his hat-covered head like he was protecting himself from marbles falling out of the sky.

As Miss Sheezley's head went inside the egg-shaped hole and she lost sight of everyone else, she must have been thinking the same thing they all were: *What diabolical weirdness has Merganzer D. Whippet planned for us next?*

One thing was for certain: They were all about to find out.

CHAPTER 9

A Floor of Fog and Mirrors

There was one large hangar in the field of wacky inventions that was used to envision and build many of the most outrageous floors of Merganzer D. Whippet's hotels. Only Merganzer's most trusted workers — a large number of whom were monkeys and robots — were allowed inside. Mr. Powell had returned with supplies and news, and as he entered the two main doors and looked every which way, he hoped it wouldn't be too hard to find the master of inventions. It was a huge space, easy to get lost in, and Powell felt overwhelmed at the sight of it all.

The ceiling was a hundred feet overhead, crisscrossed with hanging ropes and scaffolding piled in crooked stacks. Monkeys swung from some of the ropes, carrying tools or plans from one place to another. They were small but frighteningly strong and very bright. They could be taught complex tasks and master them quickly, and so they were highly useful when it came to piecing together unusual floors. Four such floors were in different stages of development in the hangar. Welding sparks flew in the distance and several rolling robots whizzed by as Powell journeyed deeper into the hangar in search of his friend.

"Merganzer? Where are you? I've returned with the supplies you requested!" Powell yelled, his voice reverberating against the far walls.

"Over here!" Merganzer yelled back. "But do approach carefully. I'm right in the middle of something rather unstable."

Merganzer was often in the middle of something unstable when he worked in the hangar, so Powell didn't seem the least bit alarmed about this news until he arrived at the metal and electric shop and saw what Merganzer was doing.

"Oh my," Mr. Powell said. "That *is* unstable."

"Hand me that Flooger, will you?" Merganzer said, reaching his one free hand out into the air. "And tear me off some duct tape. I'm going to need to shut this iron box in a second."

"What on earth would you have done if I hadn't come along when I did?" Mr. Powell asked, taking up the Flooger, which looked like a foot of orange rope, and handing it to Merganzer.

"I knew you'd arrive when I needed you. You always do."

Mr. Powell beamed with happiness. It was true. He did have a way of showing up at precisely the right time, just when Merganzer needed him the most.

"I suppose that's what friends are for," Mr. Powell said, tearing off a strip of duct tape that was just the right length and holding it out.

Merganzer was hunched over a long workbench covered with an intricate array of circuits and wires. The round Wyro, which Leo and Remi had retrieved from under the Whippet Hotel, was sitting in the middle. It was many layered and moved like a gyroscope, spinning in different directions at the same time, or so it seemed. It powered something big Merganzer needed done.

"They've just entered one of my most complicated floors sooner than I expected them to," Merganzer said. "I haven't even tested it yet!"

When he said this, a stream of goopy green liquid began streaming out of one of the tubes and the spinning Wyro began to slow down.

"As I expected," he said. "Sprung a leak!"

Merganzer wrapped duct tape around the leak in the blink of an eye and everything seemed to be working as he'd intended again.

"We're close, George. So very close!"

"You mean . . . *the AG chamber*?" Mr. Powell asked.

"Yes. I mean *the AG chamber*. I do believe the time has come at last. One of my greatest inventions is nearly ready."

"It's a good thing Leo found the Wyro. We'll need all the power it's got."

Merganzer grabbed a lever to his right and pulled it toward him. An energy dial began to move, circling closer to a clearly marked red zone as the Wyro heated up. It floated a few inches above the workbench, turning from blue to purple to red and throwing off heat Mr. Powell could feel on his face.

It all seemed very dangerous to Mr. Powell — as though an explosion with the power to destroy the universe might happen at any moment. But Merganzer appeared unconcerned. He stepped back, wiped his hands on his trousers, and asked Powell about other matters of business.

"This will take a little time," Merganzer said. "It's stable . . . for the moment. What's happening with the bids from the east?"

"The Japanese conglomerate just offered two hundred million for the furry candy."

Merganzer tapped his lengthy chin three times fast. "Hold out for two fifty and leak the offer to Nabisco."

Powell nodded. They'd been developing a frighteningly furry candy in the lab, and it was set to raise a lot of money for expansion.

"And the synthetic tooth-growing enamel? What's the counteroffer from Procter & Gamble?"

"A billion," Mr. Powell said. It was a word he loved using but didn't often have the chance.

"*And* per-unit profit sharing?"

Powell nodded. It had been a difficult negotiation, but he'd gotten that, too.

"Sell," Merganzer instructed.

There was a moment of silence between the two men in which the whirring sound of the Wyro and the glugging of the liquid in the tubes filled the space.

"I've got that feeling I get sometimes," Merganzer said. He was often capable of two expressions at once, and such was the case as he looked at his oldest friend.

"I can't tell if you're confused or concerned," Mr. Powell said, seeing both confusion and concern on Merganzer's face.

"I am both, which is not a happy combination. We must be careful as we near the end. We wouldn't want everything I've created to fall into the wrong hands."

Powell agreed, nodding, that it would be a great tragedy if the wrong person were put in charge of such important assets. But there was nothing to be done about it. If Powell knew one thing for sure, it was that Merganzer D. Whippet had his own methods for placing people in positions of power within his empire. He alone had the authority to take such risks, because he alone had masterminded the whole lot of it.

Powell wished it weren't true, but with all the worldwide plans they had before them, they had to put *someone* in charge. If Merganzer wanted to make a game of who was to hold the post, so be it. It was a gamble Powell would have to accept whether he liked it or not.

While Merganzer was busy at work in the field of wacky inventions, Leo was staring at a hazy version of himself. He stood before a wall, but it was no ordinary wall, for this one was made of mirrored glass. A thick blanket of fog swirled in the air all around him, drifting on an aimless wind.

"Merganzer, where do you get your ideas?" Leo marveled, because the wall before him was one of many such walls in the hidden floor of the Foxtrot Hotel. There were, in fact, hundreds of them. They created a labyrinth of mirrors where six different people were trapped like rats in an ever-reflecting maze.

"Remi! Lucy! Alfred!" Leo yelled, but it was no use. The fog swallowed up all the names he was saying, and everything he heard seemed far off in the distance. Voices bounced off mirrored walls, but the fog was like a sponge soaking up water: It devoured every sound, turning the whole floor into a dull roar of muted voices.

There was only one thing to be done, and that was to walk. But Leo was a very smart boy. Not only had he known how important a roll of duct tape was, and gone back to get it when it might have been lost forever, he knew he'd come upon a moment *made* for duct tape. As the fog churned all around him, he stuck the end of the roll of tape onto the mirror where he stood. Only then did he begin walking, unrolling the tape with a loud screeching sound with each step he took.

"I hope I don't get into any trouble for duct taping this mirror maze," Leo said out loud. "At least it's silver duct tape. It matches."

Leo glanced behind him and saw that his footsteps left a mark in the fog, like stepping into whipped cream. The footsteps stayed there for a few seconds, then they were eaten up by a rolling mist.

"Cool," Leo said.

He turned a corner, then another, then went down a long straight hall of mirrors until he arrived at a dead end. He ripped the tape from the roll and knew he'd need to turn back.

"Crumb," Leo said. He thought he could hear Remi's voice clearer now, and Lucy's, too. But they still sounded like they were calling from a distant shore.

"What's this?" Leo asked himself, spying something hidden in the swirling fog. He waved his hands back and forth, kneeling on the floor, and found a pile of yellow wooden blocks. Each of the blocks had a letter on one side.

"I think I better take these," Leo said, gathering all six blocks into his hands and putting them in the big front pocket of his maintenance overalls. He backtracked, following the eye-level silver line he'd already made on the mirror. When he arrived at a fork in the maze, he took out a black Sharpie and started writing on the tape: *don't go that way (arrow), do go this way (arrow)*. Then he started taping again. In this way Leo eventually bumped into Lucy, who was very excited to see him. She had also been taping and marking.

"Great minds think alike, I guess," she said, snapping the top back onto her pen with a smile.

"Have you seen anyone else?" Leo asked.

"Nope. I think they're all heading for the middle just like us, but from different parts of the floor."

Leo had noticed that the halls of mirrors were getting shorter and narrower as he went, but it hadn't occurred to him that it might be because he was getting closer to the center of the hotel.

"Did you find any of these?" Lucy asked. She held up a blue letter block, like the ones Leo had found.

"Yeah, I found a bunch of them —" He pulled them out of his pockets and held them in his cupped hands. "But mine are yellow."

Leo had six, two each of the letters *U*, *Y*, and *O*.

"I found seven," she said, looking more carefully at Leo's. "I have one weird block in my set. It has a *2x* on it. What do you think it means?"

"I bet it's a multiplier. It must mean Merganzer wants us to see your letters as two of each, like mine."

Leo examined Lucy's up close and saw that she had the letters *M*, *E*, *R*, *T*, *H*, *O*, and an extra *E*.

"Phil almost got out of my pocket about ten minutes ago," Lucy said as the little dinosaur's head popped out for a look around. "I might have never found him again in this fog."

The idea of a little dinosaur running around in a foggy maze of mirrors struck Leo as the kind of trouble that one wanted to avoid at all cost on a Merganzer D. Whippet adventure.

"Better keep a close eye on him," Leo said as they started off together. Through the use of duct tape as a sort of bread crumb trail, Lucy and Leo had come a lot farther in the maze than anyone else had. If they could have popped the top off the floor and floated far above, they would have seen that Remi, Alfred, Mr. Pilf, and Miss Sheezley were much closer to the outside edges of the hotel. In fact, Leo and Lucy turned one more corner and found themselves staring at a wall of swirling fog.

"It looks like we've arrived," Lucy said.

"What do you suppose is beyond the fog?" Leo asked. He wasn't sure he wanted to know.

"Only one way to find out," Lucy said, and she stuck her head through the fog. Leo couldn't see past her shoulders anymore. It reminded him of the headless horseman, which made him nervous, so he grabbed Lucy by her maintenance overalls and pulled her back. When he did, Phil fell out of Lucy's pocket and disappeared into the whirling mist.

"What did you do that for?!" Lucy yelled, then she dove headfirst into the wall of fog, and Leo lost sight of her entirely.

"This is getting superduper, very, totally *weird*," Leo said. He put his hand through the churning white fog, hoping to feel something on the other side that would tell him what lay hidden there. Instead, he felt like he'd put his hand sideways into a swimming pool. It turned all heavy or weightless or some indescribable combination of both.

"Lucy!" he yelled.

"Come on in!" Lucy yelled back. "Just dive — it's fine!"

Leo decided he'd rather play it a little safer than diving into a room that felt strange, so he stuck his head in, as Lucy had done. His face felt droopy and slow, and it finally struck him what was inside the room.

"It's an antigravity chamber," he said with a smile, because it was something he'd always wanted to step inside of. It was impossible, but then so was a hotel room that was also a working pinball machine. So much of Merganzer D. Whippet's world seemed *im*possible, but when you believed, it was *possible*. It would have warmed Leo's heart if he'd known the Wyro, a thing he had retrieved himself, was powering what Merganzer called *the AG chamber*.

"Help me corral Phil," Lucy said. She was floating around the room trying not to do flips and turns as she looked for Phil. The problem was the wooden blocks, which numbered in the thousands. They were floating everywhere, and even from the door Leo had to push dozens of them aside as they drifted by.

"Hang on!" Leo said. "I'm coming in!"

Leo stripped out two feet of silver duct tape and stuck it to the wall, then peeled off another two feet and dove into the antigravity room. The tape held him in one spot, where he floated as if he was in a tank full of water. He looked down for the first time and found that the wooden blocks floated all through the chamber, the bottom of which was quite a lot farther away than he was expecting.

"The bottom must be somewhere inside the floor below us, in the tiny dinosaur zoo. The antigravity must have kicked in when the two floors clicked together."

He couldn't shake the fact that the floor of the chamber was at least twenty feet below the place where they floated in the air. If the antigravity stopped working, they'd surely hit the bottom hard.

"This is the coolest thing ever," Lucy said. She was smiling from ear to ear, her ponytail lolling in circles behind her head.

"I'll have to invite you to my hotel sometime. The Whippet has a lot of stuff like this. I've got a roller coaster that will blow your mind. And a room that's a giant pinball machine. You can play it!"

"Count me in!" she yelled.

Leo looked up at the ceiling. Through the storm of wooden blocks, he saw two things: a digital clock with red numbers that was counting down, and beneath the clock, nine small squares. The clock had run down to ten minutes, but Leo had no idea what it was for.

"Hey, there's Phil! Over there!"

Phil was hugging a wooden block with all four limbs, biting into it over and over again while he did cartwheels in the air. He wasn't too far away from Leo, so Leo stripped an arm's length of tape and pushed off from the wall in Phil's direction. The sticky side of the duct tape was filling with blocks as Leo reached out as far as he could and just about grabbed Phil before Lucy yelled.

"He's pretty wound up. Better not grab him or he might bite."

"Thanks for the warning," Leo said, but he had long been a master of picking up lizards, spiders, and mice. He had an exceptional talent for that sort of thing. More important, he had a pair of hot-coal tongs he kept in one of the really long pockets of his overalls.

"Come to papa," Leo whispered, taking the tongs in hand and snapping them open and shut like a long, skinny pair of pliers. Phil was preoccupied with eating the wooden block, so when he floated just close enough, Leo had no trouble gently clamping the hot-coal tongs around Phil's waist. The tiny dinosaur was not happy. He thrashed around like a little monster caught in a trap until Lucy finally made her way back and put him in her pocket.

"Maybe give him a toy to play with," Leo said as he put away the tongs. Lucy grabbed the first wooden block to come by and dangled it next to Phil's head. He held the block with his small front claws and tried to eat it.

"Dinosaurs aren't that smart, huh?" Leo asked.

"Yeah, I'm thinking maybe that's why they're extinct," Lucy replied.

"I have a feeling I know how this puzzle works," Leo said as Lucy started to float away. He reached out his hand and she took it. There was a little zap of electricity in the air and the current ran between them, making them both laugh nervously.

"Sorry about that," Leo said.

Lucy smiled awkwardly, but kept holding his hand as they hovered in the room together. "So. The puzzle?"

"Oh, right, that," Leo stammered. "Well, I think the letters we have spell something. I've been thinking about my letters — two sets of O, *Y*, and *U* — that's gotta be two *you*s. And your letters — *M*, *E*, *R*, *T*, *H*, O, and an extra *E*. I think that spells *the more*. And you have that *2x* block, a multiplier."

"You think a lot," Lucy said.

"I know. It's a habit."

A bell seemed to go off in Lucy's head. "So we have two sets of *the more you*!"

"That we do."

"What's it mean?"

"I'm guessing the others had letter blocks on their journey, too."

Leo pointed toward the far wall, where two more openings filled with cloudy white fog swirled and moved. They both took in the four walls of the room and found a total of six such doors, one for each person in the maze.

"Hey!" Remi's voice filled the antigravity chamber, and Lucy, surprised by the noise, let go of Leo's hand. She floated out into the middle of the room, and Leo realized that she had mastered moving where she pleased. She swam toward Remi as Leo stayed stuck where he was.

"Hi, Remi — glad you could make it," Lucy said as she swam through the air. She turned her feet toward Remi and executed a ninja kick. But Remi's attention had drifted elsewhere. He was looking at the floor of the chamber, which was a long way down.

"You don't have to come inside," Leo said. He knew Remi was not the kind of person who sought out adventure unless it contained things like seat belts, donuts, and pizza.

"Oh yes, you do!" Lucy said. She had arrived at the door where Remi's head was. Putting her hand through the fog, she grabbed his red doorman's jacket and pulled him in.

"Whadja do that for?" Remi said. He was turning somersaults like an Olympic gymnast, tumbling across the room toward Leo.

"Whoa there, fella!" Leo called out. "Whoa!"

But there was no stopping Remi, who plowed through countless toy blocks and smashed into Leo. The two of them tangled and ended up back-to-back, stuck to each other with all the tape Leo had rolled into the chamber.

"You had to bring the duct tape, didn't you?" Remi said.

"Cool place, right?" Leo said, trying to wrench himself free without success as Lucy laughed.

"What on earth are you idiots doing in there?"

Miss Sheezley had arrived at her door, where her pencil-thin eyebrows were raised so high she looked like the bride of Frankenstein.

"Well, this *is* a surprise," Alfred Whitney said from the other side of the room, where he, too, had finally landed.

"Everyone just stay where you are," Leo said. "I've got this thing figured out . . . I think. I just need a second here."

He was turned upside down when he took out the box-cutting knife and began to slice away the duct tape. By the time he was free of his brother, Remi had grown used to the antigravity chamber and was laughing like a lunatic.

To everyone's surprise, Alfred Whitney jumped right in and let Comet free inside the antigravity chamber. There was never a happier duckling, for he found that his barely formed wings could carry him like a real grown-up duck. His mother would have been proud as he dodged and parried around wooden blocks, zooming through the air on moth-size wings, having the time of his little life.

"Everyone listen," Leo said, righting himself against one of the walls. "Did you find any wooden blocks in your sections of the maze?"

"I did!" Remi said. "They were green. I've got them here in my pocket with Blop."

Remi dug into his pocket and accidentally let Blop out into the open, where the small, talkative robot opened his eyes and realized where he was.

"Fascinating," he said, floating wildly in the air as wooden blocks bounced off him from every side. But that didn't stop him from speculating about the room. "Mr. Whippet worked up these plans ages ago, but I never thought he'd actually pull it together. Who gave him a Wyro?"

"We did!" Remi said joyfully. "Remember? We got it from Dr. Flart!"

"He must have fired the Wyro in the field of wacky inventions," Blop said. "The thing about a Wyro is it'll only last a little while. An hour at most."

"What's that supposed to mean?" Remi asked.

"It means this chamber isn't going to stay antigravity for much longer!" Leo yelled. "That must be what the clock is for."

"Uh-oh," Alfred said, looking up at the ceiling and seeing the clock that Leo was referring to. "If that's true, we only have six more minutes."

"Idiots," Miss Sheezley added. They could see only her head, which looked like it was detached from the rest of her body.

"Remi, what letters did you get?" Leo asked frantically.

"Let's see . . . *K, E, A,* and *T.*"

"Everyone, what's that spell if we unscramble it? Lucy and I got two sets of *the more you* with our letters."

"TAKE!" Alfred yelled. "It spells *take*!"

"Excellent!" Leo said. "And what about you, Alfred? What letters did you get?"

"Mine were purple. There were five, and I already know what they spell out: *leave.*"

"Fantastic!" Leo said. "That only leaves Miss Sheezley. Where is she?"

"I'm over here, where it's safe," she said. 'And you've got five minutes."

"I bet I know what letters she has," Lucy said. She seemed to be searching through the floating letters, trying to find certain ones. "She has *B, E, H, I, N, D.*"

"Why, she's right," Miss Sheezley said. "Clever girl."

"Looks like Leo's not the only puzzle solver in the bunch," Remi said. He was curled up in a cannonball, torpedoing through blocks.

"What are you looking for?" Leo asked Lucy.

"The answer to the riddle," she said.

"And what is the riddle?" As Alfred asked this, Comet flew right up in front of his face, showing off how talented he was, and Alfred carefully took hold of him in both hands, placing the duckling safely back inside his pocket.

"Leo and I each had two sets of the same thing — *the more you* — and the rest of you had a total of three words — *take, leave,* and *behind.*"

"So the riddle is this," Leo finished what she was saying. "The more you take, the more you leave behind."

"And the answer is *footsteps,*" Lucy said with delight. "So I'm looking for those letters. I found an *F* and an *S* so far."

Alfred piped in next. "I have an O!"

"Me too!" Remi shouted. "And a *T*!"

"I have just now grabbed another *T* out of the air," Miss Sheezley said. She was leaning out into the antigravity chamber, but she had not gone so far as to jump in. "It's the least I could do."

"We're down to three minutes," Leo said. "There are nine slots for the answer up by the clock. Everyone! To the top as fast as you can! And keep searching for another *S*, an *E*, and a *P*."

Everyone started swimming for the top. They'd all gotten used to how antigravity felt and moved with ease among the blocks. Remi swam by Blop and picked him up as he kept talking about the Wyro and gravity and how it was about to come to a stop.

"WE'RE ALL GONNA DIE!!!!" Remi screamed, looking down at the floor of the antigravity chamber, far below.

"Remi, calm down," Leo said. "There's time to finish the puzzle and get to the bottom before this thing shuts down. Come on! We need your letters!"

Lucy swam by Miss Sheezley and grabbed the letters from her hands, then arrived at the ceiling before everyone else. She placed her letters into the correct slots, where they stuck like magnets, and turned to her friends.

"Hurry! We've only got one minute left!"

Leo arrived next and put his letters in, then Alfred inserted his. The only letters they needed were an O and a *T*, and no matter how hard they searched, no one could find either. Only Remi had those letters, and he was headed for the floor, too afraid to fall and possibly break his arm, his neck, or his butt.

"I got this," Leo said. He bunched up like a ball against the ceiling and pushed off with his legs as hard as he could. It was like diving into a meteor storm in space, wooden blocks pelting him from all sides as he sliced through the room and crashed into Remi near the bottom.

"Not cool!" Remi cried out as he bounced off the floor.

"Give me the blocks, Remi! There's no time!"

Remi handed Leo the O and the *T* and watched as Leo blasted off the floor like a missile heading into outer space.

"Dang," Remi said. "My brother is awesome."

The clock ticked down to ten seconds as Leo flew.

"Get to the bottom! Fast!" he yelled.

Alfred and Lucy used the same technique Leo had used to push off the ceiling and dive for the floor. Just as Lucy was flying past the one opening no one had come out of, Mr. Pilf stepped through the door into the antigravity chamber.

"Oh my, this is bad," he said, turning every which way as he tried to understand what was happening to him. Alfred slammed right into Mr. Pilf and the two of them tumbled end over end toward the bottom, completely out of control.

At the ceiling, the clock wound down to three seconds as Leo inserted the last two letters and felt them stick to the ceiling like glue. The clock ticked down to one and then zero and then the sound of a giant energy source coming to its end was heard echoing through the antigravity chamber. Leo could feel himself start to take on weight again, but he was a very smart boy in possession of a long pair of hot-coal tongs. He gripped the tongs on a wooden block, which had a nice groove at the bottom of the letter *T*, and held on for dear life.

Remi dropped to the floor first, for he was only a foot off the ground. Lucy drifted down like a balloon running out of air as the gravity returned, landing perfectly on her feet. Mr. Pilf and Alfred were in the throes of a twisting, diving, tangled mess, from which Mr. Pilf emerged the big loser. It was he who hit the floor first, followed by Alfred, who found himself sitting on poor Mr. Pilf's rib cage.

Everyone looked up, searching for Leo Fillmore and, instead, found thousands of letter blocks falling from the sky. They rained down until Remi and Lucy found themselves hip-deep in wooden blocks and Mr. Pilf was covered entirely.

"Leo!" Lucy cried. "Hang on!"

"I'm trying!" Leo yelled back. The tongs were holding, but it was a long way to the bottom.

"I'll catch you if you fall!" Remi yelled, holding out his arms as if catching Leo were a real possibility.

The floor beneath their feet jumped wildly and everyone screamed, even Mr. Pilf, who no one could see under all the blocks.

"We're coming to you!" Alfred said. "Don't move!"

The floor was going up, toward Leo, and it was not

going slowly. It was really moving. When it arrived at the door level, which was about halfway, it stopped abruptly.

"Oh, come on!" Alfred said with frustration.

"Climb aboard, Sheezley!" Remi said, because Miss Sheezley could have stepped right onto the platform as blocks tumbled into the maze at her feet.

"No, thank you," she said, turning her nose up at Remi. "I believe one hotel will do just fine."

And with that, she was officially out of the competition. She had come to the end of her interest in having adventures.

The floor began to move toward the ceiling again, slower this time. As they looked up, everyone watched and the ceiling split apart down the middle and began to open like elevator doors. Leo was being moved to the left, swaying back and forth, when the floor and the ceiling arrived within five feet of each other.

"Let go!" Remi said, and Leo did let go.

He landed on top of the blocks, which were on top of Mr. Pilf.

"I'm under here," Mr. Pilf said in a muffled voice.

No one answered as the ceiling opened all the way and the floor moved past.

No one answered as wooden blocks tumbled off into a new room.

They didn't answer because they couldn't.

They'd just arrived inside the most magnificent Merganzer D. Whippet floor of them all, and everyone was speechless.

• CHAPTER 10 •

THE REALM OF MONDAR!

"Never send your brother to do something you could have done yourself!" Ms. Sparks said. When she was particularly upset, she spoke to the TV set. It didn't answer her back, but at least it made the sound of voices. It was something.

"Why won't he answer?!" she yelled. Then she got a little too angry and threw the special phone at the TV. It hit with a loud *ping!* and bounced onto the floor, leaving a deep scratch on the screen.

"Well, that's just perfect," she said, as if some character on a reality show had damaged her TV and she'd had nothing to do with it. She got up from the ratty couch, leaning down toward the floor as her giant beehive hairdo nearly touched the coffee table. She picked up the phone. Her eyesight wasn't very good, so she held it at arm's length, turning her nose up and squinting her eyes.

"Perhaps I dialed wrong that time," she muttered, tapping in the numbers more carefully. She got no answer, but this time, unlike the last, she did get voice mail.

She left a message.

"I've been waiting for word since morning. What's happening? If you've lost track of Leo and Remi, find them! And if you can, take them out. Nothing too violent, mind you — don't push them off a building. Tie them to a tree, something like that. I tell you, they're in cahoots with that madman Whippet. They must be stopped!"

She had gotten very loud with the message and cleared her throat, taking down her voice.

"You and I will run the Whippet Empire, as it was always meant to be. You out front, me in the shadows — he'll never know what hit him. But oh, we'll take him for all he's got, brother. You can count on that. Call me, won't you? I'm bored. Good-bye."

She tapped the END button on the phone, flopped down on the couch, and stared at the ceiling. Her tall head of hair crumpled up against the wall behind her, but she didn't care. All she cared about was getting her hands on the Whippet Empire. She thought about all the terrible things she would do from a position with that kind of power, and soon she was snoring with her mouth wide open and with the TV blaring in the background.

"Who turned out the lights?" Miss Sheezley asked.

It had become suddenly dark inside the maze of fog and mirrors when the floor of the antigravity chamber went by. She'd picked up several wooden blocks in case she needed them as weapons. She could hear sounds from above, but it was impossible to tell what they were.

"I say, can I get some light, please?" she called into the darkness. To her surprise, the request was granted in the form of a soft glow from around the corner. She followed the light, carefully and slowly, and, turning the corner, found that the light had moved. It went on like this for some time — Miss Sheezley chasing the light, the light moving somewhere else. Had she been, at that moment, in the field of wacky inventions with Merganzer and Mr. Powell, she would have been furious. The two of them were laughing their heads off, running Miss Sheezley around the maze like a mouse after a moving block of cheese.

"We really should stop," Mr. Powell finally said.

"But we're having such fun. And it's not hurting anyone. Also, she was beastly to the boys. We can't have that."

Powell looked at a table that lay before him. All the hotel floors were set out side-by-side, in miniature holograms. It was like watching a small world with real people that could be controlled and moved about.

"You know, we've had a multibillion-dollar offer for this technology," Mr. Powell said. He watched as Merganzer used a key card to turn off a light Miss Sheezley was getting close to and turn on another farther out. He laughed with a distinctly duckish quality.

"Who wants it again?" Merganzer asked.

"That Branson character. A Brit."

"Oh, now him I like," Merganzer said, rubbing his chin. "He'd make a very good telephone out of this business, wouldn't he?"

"I believe he would."

"Or a movie screen. Can you see it? Everyone sitting around the outside, a giant holographic movie in the middle? Boggles the mind."

"Yes."

"And we could invent more outrageous things with all that money!"

"Well, to be fair, you have an awful lot of money already. It's piled up all over the place. Better we spend more before we go selling anything. This Branson fellow can wait."

"We better turn our attention to the remaining competitors. Speaking of which — the girl is possibly going to be a problem."

"Lucy?" Powell said. "It all depends, I suppose, on who is left standing at the end."

Merganzer nodded slyly and tapped out a few more commands on his key card.

Miss Sheezley had become so agitated she was running toward the light, hoping to catch it before it went out. It was for this reason that she didn't notice the hole Merganzer had opened up directly around a sharp corner. It was why she slid down a long, narrow tunnel with many twists and turns. And it was why she landed in the Whippet Library, where she found Miss Harrington and E. J. Bosco.

"Pull up a chair," Bosco said. "Afternoon tea just arrived."

He had raced through all the best parts of *The Wonderful Wizard of Oz* and moved on to *Charlie and the Chocolate Factory*. On seeing the book in Bosco's hand, Miss Sheezley thought of how appropriate it was.

She was beginning to feel like she was inside a story in which Willy Wonka might pop out at any moment.

"So you're out, too?" Miss Harrington asked, sipping her tea and setting down her copy of *20,000 Leagues Under the Sea*.

"I suppose I am," Sheezley answered, sitting heavily in a soft chair and leaning back. She smiled then, looking at the tea and the cookies and the books.

"I believe I'll take a little nap, if you don't mind," she said.

She closed her eyes and relaxed, for she realized something very important just then. Even though she was not the person to run an entire empire of hotels, she loved her Foxtrot Hotel. She'd thought of little else since she'd arrived. Her task would be to make it the crown jewel of the Whippet Empire.

And so she slept peacefully, for she knew she had long since found her place in the world, which is a very good thing indeed.

"This has to be two floors, not one," Leo said, marveling at the location of the Merganzer D. Whippet Hotel where they'd arrived. Everyone but Mr. Pilf waded through the wooden blocks on the platform and looked every which way. Mr. Pilf sat up, still neck-deep in wooden blocks, and shook his head. When he saw what lay inside the floor, it crossed his mind to bury himself in blocks and hide out until the competition came to an end. He found his hat in his hand, returned it to his head, and stayed where he was.

Lucy turned in circles, taking in the whole of the place they'd all arrived in. They were all standing on Mr. Pilf's Spiff Hotel floor. E. J. Bosco's Boomtown was farther overhead, with a floor of metal grating that was shot through with many giant holes. The two floors were really one, because there was no ceiling on Mr. Pilf's hotel. MONDAR was spelled out overhead on the metal grate floor, which made it look like it was floating on air. Every corner of both floors was filled with all manner of carnival rides. And it was night inside, so all the rides were lit up with the most marvelous dancing colors. And what was more, all the rides were running.

"It's amazing how quiet it is in here," Leo said, because it was. The rides were so perfectly engineered, they made almost no sound as they moved. A complicated roller coaster snaked all through both floors, but the car running on it was whisper quiet.

Besides the roller coaster, there were at least five other rides crammed onto the two floors. All of them were dancing with lights, and all of them were already operating as if people were riding them. It was at once breathtaking and eerily quiet.

"You know what this place needs?" Alfred Whitney asked everyone. "Some screaming. These rides must be ridden."

"I believe you're right, Mr. Whitney," Leo said.

"Whoa — hold on a second." Remi, being the least adventurous of the bunch, wasn't so sure. "Let's find some carnival games first. What's the rush?"

Mr. Pilf, who had finally decided to free himself from all the wooden blocks, had come alongside them.

"I wonder if we should start there," he said, pointing to a lit pathway that lay before them like the Yellow Brick Road. It ended at the far wall of the floor, where something shaped like a refrigerator was hidden in shallow light. Above the fridge-shaped rectangle was a word written in white lights: TICKETS.

"It's as good a place as any," Lucy said. "Whatever gets us on these things the fastest. I love carnival rides!"

They moved as a group down the lit path, glancing up and down and all around as they went. Remi and Mr. Pilf were the least excited, but even they couldn't deny the wonder of it all. Merganzer D. Whippet had built a marvelous fair inside two floors of a hotel. It was certainly something to marvel at, even if getting on the rides was the one thing neither of them was hoping their adventure would include.

"There's someone in there," Leo said, stopping in his tracks as they neared the ticket office. "I think it's him."

"Him who?" Remi asked, peeking over Leo's shoulder.

"Merganzer — who else?" Leo said with a smile. He started walking again, quickening his pace as everyone followed. But when he got there, it was immediately clear that he had been wrong. There was no man inside, and certainly not Merganzer.

"It's like one of those fortune-teller games," Alfred said. "He's not real."

Now that they were all standing in front of the ticket office, they could see that it was, indeed, more like a fortune-telling machine. There was a sophisticated wooden man inside, which they could see from the waist up, but it was dark behind the glass. He looked like he was sleeping.

Without asking anyone whether or not they thought it was a good idea, Alfred tapped the end of his duck-headed cane on a weathered old button on the front of the box. The wooden man inside woke up, his eyes wide and frightening, and lights began to swirl behind the glass.

"You have awakened MONDAR, the king of this hidden realm. Do you come in peace?"

"That's just great," Remi said. "We've awakened MONDAR. Way to go, Alfred. Very nice."

"Look there," Mr. Pilf said, leaning in from behind Alfred. "You can answer him."

"You're right!" Leo said, seeing that there was a Y and an N button. "We do come in peace, don't we?"

"Let's go with no," Remi said sarcastically. "Maybe he'll blow fire in our faces."

Leo rolled his eyes. He'd known Remi long enough to understand that his brother was just nervous about going on the rides. Sarcasm was his way of coping with imminent doom.

The roller coaster zoomed past, low and upside down overhead, blowing everyone's hair sideways.

"That thing is really moving," Lucy said. "Push the *Y* already. Let's get on with it."

Leo pressed the Y button and MONDAR's head turned side to side mechanically, as if he were looking at the people assembled before him. He wore a black cape and his brilliant green eyes glowed inside his painted head.

"There is only one escape from the realm of MONDAR," he said in his deep, dramatic voice. "Rides must be ridden in the order of my choosing. Do you wish to leave my realm?"

There being no other answer that would suffice, Leo pressed the Y button again.

"So be it!" MONDAR said. "What number is in your party? One?"

"Can I press buttons for a while?" Lucy asked.

Leo stepped back and let Lucy stand before MONDAR. She pressed the N button.

"Are there two in your party?" MONDAR asked.

This went on until the number five was given.

"Do we count Blop, Comet, and Phil?" Lucy said, turning to her companions.

"I don't think so," Alfred answered. "They're not going to need seats."

"Okay, here goes."

Lucy pushed the Y button and MONDAR began to laugh slyly. As his laughter subsided, the roller coaster whished past again and Remi gulped, more nervous than ever.

"Prove to me you've mastered the realm of MONDAR!" MONDAR yelled. His voice had grown louder. "Bring me this evidence and I will set you free."

A three-by-five index card slid out of a slot on the front of MONDAR's box. Lucy pulled it out and stepped back as another card started coming out. Each of her companions then came to MONDAR and took a three-by-five ticket, examining it as he or she backed away.

"It would appear it is time to get down to business," Alfred said. "Everyone with a pocket pal, make sure he's secure. We don't want any little creatures or robots flying off a ride."

Remi looked stricken, like he might try to run away, but he held his ground as he made sure Blop was both comfortable and secure.

"Hey, it's going to be fine," Leo told his brother. "Think of all the things we've already been through. They seemed dangerous, and maybe they were. But Merganzer has never gotten us hurt. And you know what? We may never pass this way again. Better we enjoy it."

"How about if we ride together?" Lucy asked Remi. "You can scream in my face all you want. I won't mind."

"If it's all the same to you, I think I'll sit with Leo. He's my brother from another mother. We were meant to do this together."

"I bet all three of us can fit in one seat on these monsters," Leo said, smiling at the excitement that lay ahead. "Put the adults behind us — let's do this together!"

"Agreed," Alfred said, eyeing Mr. Pilf with some concern. They looked at each other accusingly, like each thought the other was hiding something.

Off they went as a group, looking at their tickets, which had been marked with three rides that needed riding. They were listed in order:

THE ZIPPER

THE FIRE BREATHER

THE TREE DRAGON

There were other rides in the realm of MONDAR — the Scorpion, Typhoon!, BLAMMO — but they were only tasked with riding these three.

The roller-coaster car zoomed by again, bringing with it a fresh gust of wind. The front of the car was carved into the head of a beastly creature.

"I'm thinking that was the tree dragon," Remi said. "Great. MONDAR saved the best for last."

When they arrived in front of the Zipper, everyone realized just how scary the ride was. There were spinning squirrel cages attached to a tall contraption that rose up into the darkness.

"I've seen this ride at fairs before," Lucy said, suddenly not so sure about it. "It's a bad one."

"Awwww, man. Did you have to say that?" Remi asked.

They found a slot in which to push their tickets

through. Leo put his in first, and felt something being driven into the cardstock. When he pulled his ticket out, there was a check mark punched onto the card.

The ride slowed down, then stopped.

Remi reluctantly punched his card, then Lucy, then Alfred and Mr. Pilf. They all pocketed their tickets as the first squirrel cage arrived in front of them.

"Time to ride!" Leo said, because he of all people in the group *loved* carnival rides. He opened the cage and slid inside on the slick seat. Lucy waited for Remi, who wouldn't move, and finally slid past him and sat down next to Leo.

"Come on, Remi," Leo called, leaning forward. "You can do this. I know you can."

Remi took a deep breath and stepped forward. Before he knew it, he'd closed the door and put on his seat belt.

"My brain is fuzzy," he said. "And I can't feel my feet."

"Calm down, buddy," Leo consoled. "We're going to be okay."

Behind them, Alfred and Mr. Pilf had also settled in.

"There's another slot on the dash," Alfred said. "But I tried it and nothing happened. I guess we need to push the button instead."

Lucy leaned forward, saw a green button on the dash, and slammed it with her fist.

"Don't go being all gentle or anything," Remi said. "Might as well make MONDAR as angry as we can."

"Totally," Lucy said, leaning back and smiling.

"No, but seriously, we probably shouldn't be hitting the rides like that," Remi said. He was going to go on about why, but the ride started, so he screamed instead.

The Zipper instantly flipped them upside down. Then the cage they were in rose to the very top of the ceiling, spinning around and around as everyone screamed. They plunged toward the floor and the cages stopped spinning. At the lowest point, they were staring at the ground, then the cages were spinning faster than before as they rose again. This went on for three revolutions before Lucy stopped laughing long enough to check on Phil, who was bouncing around inside her pocket.

"You doing okay there, little buddy?" Lucy asked, holding him firmly in her hand. Phil took one look at the situation he was in, turned in Remi's direction, and threw up. He was a tiny creature who had eaten a wooden block for lunch, so what came out looked like a spoonful of oatmeal.

It landed on Remi's cheek.

"Get it off! Get it off!" he screamed, but it was more like Elmer's Glue in its composition than anything else, and it was pretty well stuck where it had landed.

"Bummer," Leo said as they headed up for their fourth revolution, which turned out to be their last. The squirrel cages came to a stop at the bottom of the ride, but the doors did not open.

"If this thing starts up again before we get out, I'm wiping my face on your shoulder," Remi said to Lucy. But she wasn't paying any attention to Remi, she was too busy taking her ticket out of her pocket.

"The slot has lit up, you guys," she said, inserting her ticket and feeling the punch as it tore into the cardstock. When she pulled it out, there were two check marks next to THE ZIPPER.

"Go on, you two," she said. "Get your cards punched and let's get on the next ride."

Leo punched his ticket, then Remi did the same, and the door to the cage clicked open. When they got out, Alfred and Mr. Pilf were already waiting for them, looking a little worse for the wear. It's an eternal truth that adults and small dinosaurs do poorly on zipper rides. Still, Mr. Pilf was alert enough to see that Remi needed some attention. He took his spotless handkerchief out of his breast pocket and wiped away the little accident Phil had left behind.

"Thank you, Mr. Pilf. I feel much better now."

The Zipper started up again, like a ghost had punched its ticket and gotten on board.

"Come on," Lucy said. "Next up is the Fire Breather. How much fun is that going to be?!"

Even Leo thought the Fire Breather sounded outrageously dangerous, but off they went in search of the next ride. Along the way, to Remi's sheer delight, they encountered an automatic cotton candy machine. There was a lever next to the machine with three options: SMALL, MEDIUM, and HUGE. Remi pulled the lever gleefully, making sure it landed firmly on HUGE, and stood back while the machine went to work. Pink sugar shot into a round tub and a hot-air blower turned on. A mechanical arm dropped into place, holding on to what looked like a cardboard tube from a long roll of wrapping paper. A few seconds later, the tub was covered in pink cotton candy.

"That's going to be large," Mr. Pilf said. "*Very* large."

The tube of cotton candy grew larger and larger, and then the mechanical arm pulled it out of the tub and turned the treat right side up.

Remi wasted no time grabbing it before someone else did.

"It's bigger than you are," Leo said, and it was. "Good thing cotton candy weighs basically nothing."

They all ripped off pieces of cotton candy as they searched for the Fire Breather. Mr. Pilf, in a moment of unexpected goofiness, made a pink mustache and held it on with his finger, then employed his best MONDAR impression.

"You will meet your doom on the Fire Breather! DOooOooOOoM, I say!"

"He's weird," Lucy said. She was standing between Remi and Leo, and they all laughed. It was starting to feel like the best day ever, with rides and candy and adventure . . . until they found themselves staring at the Fire Breather.

"You have *got* to be joking!" Remi cried out. There was another wooden MONDAR head sitting in the middle of what looked like a gigantic hamster wheel turned on its side. The hamster wheel was spinning alarmingly fast, and MONDAR was breathing fire every five seconds. His mouth was like a flamethrower, and the fire reached all the way to the outer edge of the spinning hamster wheel.

"If you think I'm getting in that thing, you've lost your mind," Remi said.

"Oh, come on, it can't be *that* dangerous," Leo said.

"Remember the realm of gears?" Remi reminded Leo.

"What's the realm of gears?" Lucy asked.

"You'll have to come visit the Whippet to see it," Remi jumped in. "It's even more dangerous than it sounds."

Leo did sometimes wonder if Merganzer was aware of just how treacherous some of his inventions were, but he had never once in all the adventures he'd gone on felt that he was truly in mortal danger. It had always felt possible he could break an arm or have his hair singed off, but those kinds of injuries sounded cool. Just knowing it was possible to actually get hurt made everything seem like they weren't being treated like little kids. This was real adventure, the kind where you might get a black eye or lose a toe.

"Well," Leo concluded, "I'm going for it. Who's with me?"

"I am," Lucy said.

"Me too," Alfred chimed in. "This has been the best day of my life. If my suit gets scorched off, so be it. I'll buy another one."

"What if your face gets scorched off?! What then?!" Remi yelled.

"I'm taking my chances. I don't believe it's in Merganzer's nature to hurt anyone."

Mr. Pilf just shrugged. He was in, if only because he didn't want to stay inside MONDAR's realm any longer then he had to.

"Come on, Remi, think about it," Leo said. "We've been through worse. Remember the train room? And the atomic ants?"

"I really do need to visit the Whippet Hotel," Lucy said.

Remi grabbed a big wad of cotton candy and stuffed it in his mouth. Then he threw the rest like a spear, right toward MONDAR's face. MONDAR responded with a stream of fire and the cotton candy burst into flames.

"Let's do this thing," Remi said. "I'm ready."

Watching the cotton candy and the tube it was attached to go up in flames made Leo a little less sure, but he didn't say so. They all punched their tickets and the ride came to a stop. There was a latch on one part of the curved hamster wheel, and a rounded metal door swung open on quiet hinges. Everyone climbed in, and the first thing they realized was that there were no straps to hold them.

"Maybe this wasn't such a good idea after all," Leo said, but it was too late for that. The metal door slammed shut and MONDAR started talking.

"Beware my wrath! This flame is real!"

"Holy barfing dinosaurs!" Remi yelled.

The giant wheel began to turn like the inside of a washing machine on spin cycle.

MONDAR's head spun one way, then the other. His emerald eyes grew larger in his wooden head, a few seconds passed, and he blew a line of fire that just missed Lucy as she tumbled out of the way.

"Lucy!" Leo yelled.

The wheel was moving much faster now, so fast that everyone was held to the curved wall by gravity.

"I'm okay!" Lucy said, standing on the grated metal underfoot. "He looks one way, then the other. Then his eyes get bigger —"

"Then it's flamethrower time," Remi said.

"That's right!" Alfred agreed.

Unfortunately for everyone on the ride, the Fire Breather had reached its optimal speed, otherwise known as *face-melting fast*. The floor fell out from under them, but the gravity kept them all stuck to the wall.

MONDAR laughed maniacally. His head spun one way, then the other. Then he stopped and his eyes got real big.

"Mr. Pilf! Get out of the way!" Leo yelled. MONDAR's face was pointing right where Mr. Pilf was standing. He curled into a ball at the bottom of the hamster wheel and the flame shot directly over his head.

"I smell something burning," Remi said. "That can't be good."

Alfred rolled along the wheel until he came to Mr. Pilf. Mr. Pilf's hat had caught fire, but Alfred had it out in a jiffy.

"Thank you, Alfred," Mr. Pilf said, working his way back into a standing position. "I do so like this hat. I'm glad it's not been completely ruined."

"My pleasure."

Remi had figured something else out during his time in the hamster wheel.

"Stop, drop, and roll," he said.

"What are you talking about?" Leo asked.

"From school — stop, drop, and roll. Everyone stay standing even though there's no floor to stand on. If a flame is coming toward you, just roll out of the way. It's easy."

As if to prove Remi's point, MONDAR blew a flame directly in Remi's direction and Remi gamely rolled his round body to one side, avoiding harm.

After that, the ride was a lot more fun. They bumped into one another a couple of times and that made it scarier, but they knew how to stay out of MONDAR's fire breathing. After a while the floor returned and the ride slowed down. When it stopped, a sliver of light poured out of MONDAR's head and he spoke.

"Tickets please."

Everyone walked up to MONDAR and slid their tickets into the top of his head so they could be punched.

"Next up, the Tree Dragon!" Remi said, exiting the ride and looking both ways.

"It takes him a little while to get warmed up," Leo whispered to Lucy. "But once he's in, he's *all* in."

"So I see," she said. Her hand brushed against Leo's, and for the briefest moment they both held on. When he let go, Leo asked Lucy if she would sit next to him on the Tree Dragon. She smiled, nodded, and ran after Remi in search of their next destination.

They passed by the rides that were not on their tickets. The Scorpion was a wicked-cool slide they all wished they could ride, and Typhoon! looked so complicated they weren't even sure how one got on. And there was BLAMMO, which involved giant spinning paddles and bungee cords. But they had tickets for only one more ride, the Tree Dragon, the great roller coaster in the realm of MONDAR.

Where it would lead them, they could not know.

But they knew they were very near the end of their adventure.

Only the top floor of the new Merganzer D. Whippet hotel remained, and though they could not have known, it was already on the move in the sky outside.

• CHAPTER 11 •

The Voyage of the Tree Dragon

Roots as thick as telephone poles snaked all through the realm of MONDAR, but they were especially thick on the second level of the floor, where the party of five stood. Getting to the top half of the realm of MONDAR had required some adept climbing, especially for Alfred Whitney. His bum knees made the effort all the more challenging, but his fighting football spirit returned, and he gladly made his way up with the others. It required some swinging from vines, which the boys and Lucy enjoyed and the adults endured. But, eventually, through much backtracking, swinging, and climbing, they'd reached the grated metal floor of the upper level.

"It's like a forest up here," Lucy said, and it was. The roots sprung up into great trees full of leaves, but Leo had long since begun to wonder if any of it was actually alive. He retrieved a hammer from his maintenance overalls along with a Phillips screwdriver. The Tree Dragon whished by on tracks that looked like long limbs as Leo pounded the screwdriver into the side of one of the trees.

"As I suspected," Leo said, a piece of the tree breaking free and falling onto the grated metal floor. "There's no way a tree could grow in here. It's all made out of something else."

Remi picked up the piece of the tree that had broken free and brought it to his bulbous nose, sniffing it. Then he licked it.

"It's candy," Remi said. "Tastes like butterscotch."

"Astounding," Alfred said, leaning in close to the tree and licking it.

"Sometimes you act like a big kid," Remi said. "Anyone ever tell you that?"

"Not often enough. I take it as a compliment, thank you."

"Think nothing of it." Remi shrugged.

"Shouldn't we be getting on with this?" Mr. Pilf said, even though he couldn't help but steal a snack as well. "It looks like we board over there, next to the moon."

A moon had been built on one of the far walls of the floor, where it glowed as though it were real. Fireflies danced all around it, buzzing in circles.

"He's right," Lucy said. "We really should get out of the realm of MONDAR as quickly as we can. And the only way out is to punch these tickets with our last ride. Come on, let's do it."

Everyone moved as one toward the shimmering moon until they reached the final slot for their tickets. One by one they had their tickets punched and the Tree Dragon car came to a stop in front of them. There were two rows of seats, and the front was filled with two boys and a girl before either adult had a thing to say about it.

"I guess we're in back again," Mr. Pilf said. "Okay by me."

The Tree Dragon was not a ride to be trifled with — that much was clear to everyone when a thick metal rail covered in foam settled firmly across their laps. There was no getting out of the Tree Dragon until it decided to let its riders go.

"Everyone ready?" Leo asked.

A collection of yeses and one maybe from Remi ensued, and Leo pushed the green button on the dashboard. They were locked in, and all of them were about to ride the Tree Dragon to its final destination whether they liked it or not.

"Here we go!" Lucy yelled, raising her arms in the air. Phil, who was peeking out of her pocket, did the same. He was a copycat.

Remi had taken special care not to sit next to Lucy in case there was another projectile vomiting event from Phil.

"Good luck with that," Remi said, smiling at Leo, who sat in the middle.

"Thanks, buddy. I appreciate it."

The Tree Dragon began to move very slowly, jerking forward in small bursts like it was struggling to get started again. A distant cry of maniacal laughter filled the air, and the shadow of MONDAR covered the rising moon.

"Does that seem like a bad omen to anyone besides me?" Remi asked.

There was no time for an answer between Remi finishing his question and the Tree Dragon bursting forward like it was propelled by jet fuel (which, Leo would later discover, was actually true). Alfred and Mr. Pilf gripped the rail over their legs with white knuckles, holding on for dear life as their heads snapped back.

The Tree Dragon rolled on rails that looked for all the world like they were part of the roots and trees themselves. It was a tangled mess of a track, but somehow the coaster stayed on as it headed straight for a wall and banked sharply down and to the right. As quick as it was heading down, it was shooting up in a spiral, then gliding upside down across the high ceiling of the hotel.

"Hold on to Blop!" Leo yelled. "And Comet! And Phil!"

There were lots of pocket buddies to worry about as the Tree Dragon dove once more, heading straight for the ticket office on the first floor and banking left in the nick of time. Mr. Pilf's hat flew off and he screamed, but Alfred was extremely quick for a man of his age, especially with his cane. He reached out, caught the inside of the hat with the tip of his cane, and slowly drew it back in before it got away for good.

"Better hold on to that!" Alfred yelled, his hair blowing back and tears running sideways out of the corners of his eyes.

"Thank you, Alfred! That's twice you've saved my favorite hat!"

"Think nothing of it—" Alfred said, then they were flipping around in circles like a corkscrew, screaming in each other's faces.

"The old dudes are having a time, aren't they?" Leo said to his two friends in the front seat.

"Me toooooooo," Lucy howled as they turned a wide, fast curve along a far wall.

The Tree Dragon had gone all the way around the entire course of tracks, and when they came back to the place where everyone had gotten on, the roots before them moved to the right.

"I think we're heading onto a different set of tracks," Leo said. "Maybe we're almost done."

Smoke billowed out of the Tree Dragon's nostrils, filling the air like a choo-choo train, and it banked up onto the wall, turning sharply. It stayed that way, riding in a wide circle around the edge of the hotel, gaining speed with each rotation.

"We're going faster!" Remi said. The skin on his chubby cheeks pushed back against his ears as the gravity increased, and the slot for punching their tickets lit up green on the dash.

"Time to punch our tickets!" Lucy yelled, and everyone struggled to get their tickets out of their pockets. Leo got there first, then Lucy, and finally Remi. In the backseat, Mr. Pilf went first, and then Alfred Whitney punched the last ticket of the bunch.

The Tree Dragon glanced down sharply, driving straight through the middle of the floor.

"We're heading for the wall!" Remi yelled. "And there's MONDAR!"

The tracks they were on appeared to end at the far wall, and the Tree Dragon wasn't slowing down.

If anything, it was gaining even more speed. The dragon breathed fire for the first time, illuminating MONDAR's face painted on the wall they were blasting toward.

"Now you leave the realm of MONDAR!" a voice boomed into the hotel.

They were on a crash course with the hotel itself, fire billowing along the sides of the coaster as they went faster still.

"I'll miss you, bro!" Remi yelled.

The Tree Dragon hit the wall with incredible force, blasting a hole in the building big enough for a car to drive through. It was very lucky then, for everyone on board, that Merganzer D. Whippet had laid a great deal more track outside his hotel than inside.

"Hey! We're still alive!" Remi laughed.

"So that's what these were." Leo smiled, for they were riding on rails that looked like tree limbs, the very ones they'd seen when they first arrived. The Tree Dragon swooped down to the ground, then up into the air, where they rode along the canopy of trees. Turning sharply and heading back into the middle, they saw the top of the new Merganzer D. Whippet hotel for the first time. It was the only thing that sat higher than the trees, and as they passed by, Merganzer himself waved from the roof.

“Lovely ride, isn’t it?” he asked them as they sped by.

“The best!” Leo answered, and then they were diving again, winding through the trees and into the field of wacky inventions. They circled the tents and buildings, then rose a final time, past the trees, to the highest point of the ride. There it slowed dramatically at its curved apex, and they saw the grandeur of all Merganzer D. Whippet had accomplished. The tents were massive and colorful, like something out of a circus, and the buildings lay clustered like tiny German villages gathered against the cold. It was a fairy-tale scene of stone spires shooting up through green and golden leaves. Pathways of red and yellow wound about the ground below, like strings of colored yarn pulled free from the warmest blanket in the world. It was a place of invention and magic, of dreams and laughter. It was, quite possibly, the best place on earth.

“I’m glad I made it this far,” Mr. Pilf said. “If only to see this, the one time.”

“Ditto,” Remi said.

“I wonder if this is the end?” Lucy asked. A split second later, the Tree Dragon was billowing steam again, breathing fire into the open sky.

“Looks to me like the tracks end down there, on the roof,” Leo said.

The Tree Dragon rolled back into action, riding a corkscrew of turns down, down, down to the level of the hotel. It came to a stop next to Mr. Powell and Merganzer, who stood waiting for them.

"Now then, wasn't that refreshing?" Merganzer asked.

"I suppose that's one way of looking at it," Alfred said.

"Ahh, Mr. Whitney! So glad to find you still afoot!"

"I as well, sir," said Alfred, breathing a big sigh of relief for having survived the perilous journey to the roof of the new Merganzer D. Whippet hotel.

The safety rails released, but no one got out, not right away. They were wondering, mostly, what Merganzer would make of Lucy.

Merganzer seemed to read their minds.

"I see you have a stowaway with you."

"We do, sir," Leo jumped in. He wanted to defend Lucy for all her bravery, but Merganzer held up his hand.

"Let's all go inside first," Merganzer said. "This will be easier to figure out with some cookies and milk."

"Agreed," Remi said. "Everything is easier to figure out with cookies and milk. It's a known fact."

And so everyone disembarked from the Tree Dragon and followed Merganzer across the roof of his new private hotel, which was now complete.

There had been a lot of ups and downs and sideways on the ride. Lots of bouncing around.

It was hard to say where something like a satellite phone might end up after a ride like that. But either way, it would soon be ringing, and someone would surely pick it up.

• CHAPTER 12 •

AN EMPEROR IS CHOSEN

Leo didn't want to leave the roof as the Tree Dragon rolled away, starting its journey back to the realm of MONDAR. He stayed at the very end of the line, hoping for more time to survey the panoramic view. Turning in a slow circle, Leo saw that the roof of the Merganzer D. Whippet was just like the roof of the Whippet back home. It was clear to Leo that Merganzer liked this kind of roof, with a garden and a pond and plenty of ducks.

The rest of the party stopped short and turned back, because Betty was waddling around the edge of the circular pond, honking like a lunatic.

"She's been in a mood all day," Merganzer called back. "I can't seem to calm her down. She won't even eat animal crackers."

"Let's get her back together with you-know-who," Alfred said. He dug down into his pocket and pulled out Comet, setting him on the ground. The little duckling honked happily and ran to its mother and siblings. Betty took one look at Comet and began quacking and waddling, drawing Comet into the fold. Everyone who was there that day would later agree that mother ducks are, on very rare occasions, known to smile.

"Well," Merganzer marveled. "Nothing like a mother duck with her long-lost duckling."

"He's a bit of a roamer," Alfred explained. "We found him on the roof of the Whippet, but really, it was my fault. I tempted him with granola bars."

"Granola bars, you say?" Merganzer asked. "Well, if they like those, I'll start making them. Healthier than animal crackers."

Merganzer pulled an animal cracker out of his own pocket and tossed it in the air, catching it on his tongue and crunching it down.

"How about that milk and cookies?" he said with a twinkle in his eye. "Fresh-baked chocolate chip."

They came to a ladder at the edge of the roof and went down, one after the other, arriving inside the top floor of the new Merganzer D. Whippet hotel. It was a wonderful open room, filled with dozens of tall, rectangular pedestals. A winding pathway ran between them all, and Merganzer explained what each one was.

"These are some of my many treasures. They're holograms, something I've cooked up so I can keep an eye on everything."

The top of each pedestal had a replica of a hotel floor. It was like a four-dimensional view of each location, with people moving about and everything.

"I avoid the rooms where people are staying, for obvious reasons," Merganzer explained. "But everything else is here, for me to keep an eye on. I am always watching, always tinkering."

"Hey!" Remi shouted. He was up on his toes, getting a better look at the top of one of the pedestals. "It's the realm of MONDAR. And there's the Tree Dragon. It's back!"

Sure enough, the coaster had rolled back to its home, where it parked in the loading zone and waited for the next rider to appear with a ticket to be punched. Watching all this happen in miniature was just plain fantastic. It wasn't like watching television; it was as if the entire floor was sitting right there, shrunk down but very real, a world unto itself.

Merganzer reached his hand inside, cutting through the light of the hologram, and pointed out the different rides.

"When I was a boy, my mother took me to Coney Island. Just one time, that's all, but I never forgot what fun it was. The rides, the cotton candy, the thrill of it all. I've been working on my own rides ever since."

"You're like Walt Disney!" Remi said. "You should open a real theme park. Kids would go nuts for this stuff."

There was a mischievous glimmer in Merganzer's eyes, as if he were already planning just such a venture.

"I'll get the cookies and the milk; you can all look around a little bit."

Merganzer raced off, as excited as a child on Christmas morning, and everyone else spread out, searching the floor for more treasures.

"Look here, Mr. Pilf," Alfred said. "It's the lobby of your hotel."

"So it is," Mr. Pilf said as they both gazed down into the Spiff Hotel, which had a very spiffy lobby indeed. "It's busy there today. I hope the staff is managing without me."

Leo found the Whippet and enjoyed looking down at Captain Rickenbacker as he stalked the gardener, Mr. Phipps, out on the grounds. He'd been away only a couple of days, but already he missed his beloved hotel. Lucy found the realm of gears and couldn't believe her eyes.

"You two were in there while those things were moving?" she asked as Remi and Leo came near. Even small and unmoving, the gears looked like a hazardous place to wander around in search of clues.

"Loved that place," Remi said, shaking his head slowly. "And Clyde, that mechanical dog. And Dr. Flart. Good guys."

"Time to get down to business," Merganzer called from the far end of the room. There were five fancy chairs lined up in a row, all of them facing a table with a big tray of cookies and glasses of cold milk. And there was one more chair, a green furry one, where Merganzer was seated, waiting for them.

"Take a treat, if you like," he said. "And please, sit. It's been a long day."

Warm chocolate chip cookies and cold glasses of milk were picked up, and each person settled into a chair.

"And so our meeting comes to order," Merganzer said. "Let me begin by saying how surprised I am to see so many of you here. It was a complicated challenge getting this far, one that required more than just puzzle-solving skills and bravery. No one makes it this far on his or her own, so you each have at least some team-building ability. And you're all leaders, to some degree. Those things are important if you're trying to run not one but six of the finest hotels in the world."

"Could I just say, for the record, that I don't want to run six hotels," Lucy offered.

Merganzer tilted his head to the left and looked at Lucy sideways. He seemed to be sizing her up, determining her weight, counting the fingers on each of her hands.

"I've been watching you," Merganzer finally said. "For a lot longer than you probably know. You remind me of Leo, a very clever and handy young man."

"I am handy," Lucy said. "That's true."

"And brave," Merganzer said, turning his gaze on the plate of chocolate chip cookies. "Let's not rule anyone out, not just yet."

There were, quite clearly, things to be discussed as they pertained to Lucy. She had, after all, been a stowaway in the tiny dinosaur zoo, hiding out from her crummy foster parents. And she was in possession of a T. rex named Phil, which she was hiding in her pocket. It would all need to be discussed, and Alfred was just about to voice his own opinions on the subject, when a strange sound was heard.

Mr. Pilf, who had been rather quiet since his arrival in the treasure room, turned to Alfred, who was sitting next to him. He didn't say a word, but his face registered surprise.

"Someone's pocket is ringing," Remi said through a mouthful of cookie.

"It must be a special sort of phone," Merganzer said. "Normal ones won't work here. I've made sure of that. Too distracting, can't get anything done with phones going off all the time."

Alfred let the phone ring a few more times — it was set to vibrate, so it buzzed softly in his pocket.

"Does anyone mind if I answer it?" Alfred asked.

"I didn't even think phones were allowed," Mr. Pilf protested. "I think Alfred should be disqualified. If it *is* some sort of special phone, he might have been getting hints along the way."

Merganzer pulled on his ear lobe with a long gloved hand and leaned forward.

"How about if I answer it for you?" Merganzer asked, holding his hand out into the air.

Mr. Pilf didn't like that idea one bit.

"But he's a cheat! Why not send him and his phone packing and get on with it?"

"There's no rush here," Merganzer stated flatly.

"We've got all day if we need it. Mr. Whitney, if you please."

Alfred removed the phone, which was still buzzing in his hand, from his pocket and gave it to Merganzer. There was some fumbling with the screen as he put the call on speaker, so everyone could hear.

"Yes?" Merganzer said in an old Hollywood low voice. He was astonishingly good at impressions, and his effort at Alfred was spot-on.

"Roger? Is that you? Blow your nose, you sound like a moose."

Merganzer, Leo, and Remi were immediately aware of who the caller was. Ms. Sparks had a very distinct, distressingly high-pitched voice.

Merganzer put a finger to his lips, which was good, because Remi was just about to ask who Roger was.

Merganzer looked at Mr. Pilf with a certain kind of sadness, then his voice changed, and his impression of Mr. Pilf was every bit as good as his impression of Alfred.

"Things have taken a turn for the worst, I'm afraid," Merganzer said in Mr. Pilf's voice.

"Why am I not surprised?" Ms. Sparks yelled. "You incompetent fool!"

The real Mr. Pilf turned red-faced. He looked like he wished he could disappear.

"I dislike it when you talk to me that way," Merganzer said in Mr. Pilf's voice. "Why must you be so negative all the time?"

"Why couldn't I have had a sister?" Ms. Sparks asked. "Little brothers are *so* pathetic. Tell me what's happening and I'll tell you what to do."

Leo and Remi exchanged a glance. Mr. Pilf? Mr. Roger Pilf was Ms. Sparks's little brother? Remi leaned in close and whispered in Leo's ear, "Can you imagine what his childhood was like? Poor guy."

Leo nodded. He felt less betrayed by Mr. Pilf than sorry for him. Mr. Pilf hadn't seemed like such a bad guy. He was a little bit of a coward, but who wouldn't be with a tyrannical sister like Ms. Sparks?

"I've made it to the very end of the competition," Merganzer said. "Unfortunately, I'm not the only one."

"Those meddling kids," Ms. Sparks snapped.

"Also Mr. Alfred Whitney," Merganzer went on in Pilf's voice.

"He can barely walk! *And* he's as dumb as a tube of toothpaste."

Mr. Pilf made a pained expression. This was turning very embarrassing, and fast.

"In any case," Merganzer said, "they're all sitting here with me. Would you like to say hello?"

"This is no time for jokes," Ms. Sparks said. She paced the grubby carpet in her shabby apartment and let loose on Roger Pilf. "Might I remind you that *I* run this show, not you, little brother. It was me who prepared all the documents to legally change your last name, me who concocted that preposterous résumé of yours. Ha! You were a waffle-eating numbskull living here, in this rathole of an apartment, before I got you that job. You were no high-flying hotel manager from Canada! Have you forgotten that was all manufactured by *me*? I made sure you were hired to run the Spiff. *You owe me.*"

The real Mr. Pilf stood up, wringing his hands as his face shook with anger.

"He does look a little bit like her," Leo leaned close to Remi and said. "The eyes, that nose."

Mr. Pilf ran over to the phone and let decades of anger and resentment out for everyone, especially his sister, to hear. "I've had it up to here with you badgering me into doing whatever you tell me to do!" he yelled. "I'm telling Mom!"

"Oh no you don't!" Ms. Sparks said. "She thinks you're as worthless as I do!"

"I quit!" Mr. Pilf said. "I quit the competition and I quit as manager of the Spiff Hotel!"

"Brat," Ms. Sparks said. "Brat, brat, brat!"

The situation was starting to spin wildly out of control, and that's when Merganzer used his real voice to bring two temper tantrums to a close.

"Ms. Sparks, it's me, Merganzer D. Whippet."

A deadly silence fell over the room.

"I'm afraid we have some important work to do here," Merganzer went on. "I'm going to need to cut this conversation short."

Mr. Pilf walked right up to Merganzer D. Whippet and ripped the satellite phone from his hands.

"Good-bye, Lenora!"

He had called her by her first name, which Ms. Sparks hated with every fiber of her being. She was screaming into the phone on her end, but no one inside the treasure room at the new Merganzer D. Whippet hotel could hear her. Mr. Pilf had dropped the phone, smashing it over and over again with the heel of his boot.

"That is one angry little man," Remi said, biting into his cookie like he was eating snacks and watching a movie.

"Mr. Pilf," Merganzer said quietly, "might I have a word with you, privately?"

Mr. Pilf was breathing heavily, but he calmed down at the soothing sound of Merganzer's voice. The two of them walked to the far side of the floor, where words no one else could hear were exchanged.

When they were through, Mr. Pilf turned to the group.

"I'm sorry, truly I am. You deserve better. I hope you can forgive me."

Mr. Pilf stood beside a gold fireman's pole, and after a formal handshake with Merganzer, he looked back at the rest of the group once more. He nodded, gave a half smile, and grabbed hold of the pole. Then he jumped into the hole and started sliding, on his way to the library below, where he would be reunited with all the other hotel managers who had been disqualified from the competition.

"How did you come to have the phone?" Merganzer asked Alfred.

"It kept buzzing in Mr. Pilf's pocket on the rides in the realm of MONDAR. We were seatmates on that part of the adventure, so it wasn't hard to miss. I suppose Ms. Sparks was a little too curious for her own good."

"Well, it was a very nice piece of sleuthing, Alfred. Well done."

"Thank you, sir."

"And don't worry too much about our Mr. Pilf," Merganzer went on. "It can't be easy having an older sister the likes of Ms. Sparks. He won't be running the

Spiff, but I'll find something for him to do here, in the field of wacky inventions. I have a feeling he's ready for a change of scenery."

"That's very fair of you, sir. Vary fair indeed."

"Everyone deserves a second chance, don't you think?"

"I do."

Merganzer looked longingly at his watch, as if he wished he were already working on a theme park or a new invention or some other very big thing.

Leo stood up from his chair.

"I've got something to say."

He looked at Lucy and smiled, then at his best friend and brother, Remi. And finally his gaze landed on Alfred, who had been so much help during their journey to the top of the new Merganzer D. Whippet hotel.

"I'm only a kid," Leo began. "And, to be honest, I'm kind of attached to the Whippet Hotel. I don't think I'm ready to run the Whippet Empire. But I think someone else is."

"Go on," Merganzer said, sitting down in his furry green chair with a look of curiosity on his face.

"Alfred Whitney exhibited bravery, leadership, and teamwork from beginning to end. He's your man. He should be running the Whippet Empire."

"And he knows how to care for a duckling," Lucy said. "I second the nomination."

"Can we come back and visit the dinosaurs and ride the rides even if Leo isn't the winner?" Remi asked.

Merganzer didn't answer right away. He looked at Leo, long and thoughtful, then at Alfred, who was resting both palms on his duck-headed cane.

"What do you say, Alfred?" Merganzer asked, not sure if the manager of the Paddington Hotel was up for the much bigger job.

"It would be a great, great honor to serve you in this way, Mr. Whippet," Alfred said. "But I do have one condition, and I'm afraid it's non-negotiable."

Merganzer raised an eyebrow. "Do tell."

Alfred turned in his chair so that he was facing Lucy.

"I can't claim that I've ever had a wife or children, so I don't really know what I'm doing. And I had a tough go of it there for a while, after my days on the football field. I was aimless, a little sad — lost, I suppose. And then someone by the name of George Powell found me at work as the doorman at the Paddington. He took a great interest in my future. It took a lot of work and a long time, but eventually, he asked me if I would manage that fine hotel."

"Hey! I'm a doorman!" Remi shouted. "Maybe I'll run a hotel someday."

Everyone smiled, because even Lucy knew that Remi had a long way to go before he was ready to run a hotel.

"Mr. Whippet's hotel has been my whole life these many years, and I've been very happy there," Alfred went on. "But what I'd really like, what would make me so very happy, would be if you, Lucy, would come with me. Will you do that?"

Lucy started to cry. She was not the crying type, so looking back and forth among all her new friends, she also laughed, wiping her face as the tears came down.

"I'm handy," she said.

"I know you are," Alfred said. "You would be so much help to me."

"And you can come visit us at the Whippet whenever you want!" Leo said, maybe a little too excitedly.

"You like this girl or what?" Remi joked, but it was true. Leo was smitten.

Lucy couldn't stop smiling even as the tears kept running down her face in little tracks. She nodded, and Alfred gave her a hanky from his jacket pocket.

"My only condition is that you help me adopt Lucy," Alfred said to Merganzer. "I'm going to need her to help me run all these hotels properly."

Merganzer smiled one of his very big smiles.

"I do like your cane," he said. "Wherever did you get it?"

"From you, of course. Don't you remember? It was my holiday present only last year."

"Oh yes, I suppose I did give it to you," Merganzer said slyly. "Have you ever taken the top off to see what's inside?"

Alfred examined his cane, then took the golden duck head in one hand and tried to turn it.

"You'll need to turn it harder than that," Merganzer said.

Alfred's hands were a little on the old side and sometimes didn't grip as well as he'd hoped they would.

"Lucy, could you open this for me?" he asked.

Lucy wiped the last of her tears and took the cane without hesitation. She dug around inside her maintenance overalls and found two pairs of rubber-coated pliers.

"These are the best. They don't leave scratches on doorknobs and kitchen handles."

"I could use some of those," Leo said, for he liked interesting tools every bit as much as Lucy did.

She had one set of pliers on the cane itself and the other on the golden duck head in no time flat. A few gentle torques and she'd broken the seal and the head was spinning. She put her tools back in her pockets and handed the cane back to Alfred.

"It's ready for you now," she said.

Alfred nodded with a grin and turned the duck head round and round until it came apart from the cane. When he lifted it off, there was a long, thin neck attached. He handed the cane to Lucy to hold, and turned the gold neck of the duck sideways, for there were words engraved there.

"'The keeper of this cane is,'" Alfred started. He had to turn the neck to read the rest, and as he did, Merganzer finished the message for him: "'Emperor of all Whippet hotels.'"

Alfred blushed.

"It's a bit over the top, don't you think?" he said.

"Completely," Merganzer agreed. "But president just sounds so . . . ordinary."

"But why did you give it to me all those months ago?" Alfred asked.

"Because I knew, long ago, that you were the man for the job. You've been very good to me, Alfred. You've earned it. I just knew you'd prove yourself loyal and trustworthy in a competition such as this. And I had some hope, where Lucy was concerned, so there was that."

Now Alfred was starting to cry, but it wasn't because he'd been put in charge of the Whippet Empire.

"I never would have guessed there was so much treasure in the world."

Alfred looked at Merganzer like the true friend he was, then his gaze fell on Leo and Remi, whom he trusted completely, and finally on Lucy, the real fortune in the deal.

Merganzer knelt down next to Lucy and watched as Phil popped his head out and looked around. He'd awoken from a nap and let out a hilarious T. rex yawn.

"I'm afraid Phil will need to go back to his home," Merganzer said. "He'll be safer there. But you can come visit. I hope you will."

"And ride the Tree Dragon?" she asked hopefully.

"And ride the Tree Dragon, of course," Merganzer replied, looking up at Remi and Leo. "What fun would the rides be if there were no children to enjoy them?"

When Mr. Pilf landed in the library, he found all the other hotel managers sitting in cozy chairs, reading books and sipping tea. He had expected to see them bickering, climbing up the walls with boredom, and possibly throwing punches at one another. Hotel managers could be unpredictable when they were forced to spend time locked in a room together, but he had to admit, they were acting . . . unpredictably.

"Hello, everyone. I've just arrived by sliding down a firehouse pole. Also, I did not win the competition."

Miss Harrington, who had earlier tricked Mr. Pilf into searching for her hat, looked up from her book. Her dark hair was up in a bun, like a librarian, and she was wearing reading glasses. For an instant, Mr. Pilf thought she looked older than before, and this he liked.

"I'm relieved you won't be our boss. Can you tell us who will be?"

"Probably that kid, Leo Fillmore," Mr. Pilf said. "He's very resourceful."

"Really?" Miss Sheezley asked. She sipped her tea like a princess, setting her book across her lap.

"Or Alfred," Mr. Pilf said. He flopped down in the one remaining chair and picked up the first book that caught his eye.

"*A Wrinkle in Time*," he said, stroking his long, thin beard. "By Madeleine L'Engle. I haven't read a book in ages."

"It's not so easy at first," E. J. Bosco said, harrumphing as if he had a whole shrimp stuck sideways in his throat. "During the first hour you'll fall asleep at least four times. After that it gets easier, more relaxing."

"I do wish Alfred would take over," Miss Harrington said. "He seems the most suited to the task. And who wants to be managed by a kid? That sounds intolerable."

Mr. Pilf shrugged, flipping to the first page of *The Thin Man*. "I'm not sure it's going to matter for me. I'm probably out of the hotel business."

"But why?" Miss Harrington asked. She looked stricken, like one of those women who covers her feelings for someone by treating them like dirt.

"It's a long story that would probably make a good book," Mr. Pilf said. "Full of deceit and dastardly plots and monstrous characters."

"Oooh," Miss Sheezley said. "And is there some romance in there? Because if there is, I'll read it."

"I'm afraid there's no romance," Mr. Pilf said.

"None whatsoever? Not even a scrap?" Miss Harrington asked wistfully.

Mr. Pilf and Miss Harrington looked at each other as if maybe there would be a little romance in Mr. Pilf's story after all, and that alone made him feel quite a lot better.

"I believe I'll read a little bit about this thin man and see what I think," Mr. Pilf said. He glanced at E. J. Bosco, who had fallen asleep like a walrus on a beach.

"Tea?" Miss Harrington asked, holding the pot.

"Don't mind if I do," Mr. Pilf answered.

And then he and all the rest of the hotel managers who were still awake kicked their feet up and lost themselves entirely in the books they were holding.

It was the first of many reading vacations they would share together on orders from the new head of the Whippet Empire.

· CHAPTER 13 ·

BEYOND THE FIELD OF WACKY INVENTIONS

In the four months that followed the competition, a great many people speculated about what Merganzer D. Whippet was busy working on. Even Leo Fillmore, who was widely regarded as one of Merganzer's very closest friends, didn't have the slightest idea what Merganzer had been up to. No one had been invited back to the field of wacky inventions, and no one had tried to find their way back to the place where a remarkable hotel had been built in a day.

And so it was that a party in which Merganzer was the special guest was bound to be met with profound curiosity. What had he been doing all those months? Was he building another hotel in the South of France?

Or maybe he was busy developing new rides for that theme park everyone hoped he would build. Or inventing things like furry candy, antigravity rooms, and tiny dinosaurs.

It was impossible to say.

Mr. Fillmore and Pilar were putting the finishing touches on decorations around the Whippet Hotel grounds.

"I'm very glad he chose to have a party here. Is exciting, no?" Pilar asked.

"I'm just happy the Whippet is running smoothly and the boys didn't break anything this week."

Mr. Fillmore was the head maintenance man, and while Leo was not a breaker of many things, his brother made up for it in spades. Leo often took blame for things Remi broke in the hotel, just to even things up a little.

The sun was down and thousands of lights, strung by Mr. Phipps, the gardener, were draped around the grounds. All the bushes carved into the shapes of animals were covered in blankets of white lights, and the pond was alive with floating paper lanterns.

"So you really have no idea why he's coming out of hiding?" E. J. Bosco cracked open a fortune cookie, one of many in a big glass bowl on a table, and tossed the crumbled pieces into his mouth.

"None whatsoever," Miss Sheezley said. She was carrying a tote bag full of books she'd brought to hand out, things she'd read and loved in recent weeks. She had her eye on the new manager of the Spiff, a regal, fully bearded gentleman by the name of Fitzpatrick, and wandered off in order to give him a book she'd picked out for him. He was Scottish — that much she knew — and she'd purchased a rare first edition of *The Expedition of Humphry Clinker* (the name alone was a conversation starter).

E. J. Bosco opened his fortune and read it to Alfred, who stood next to him.

"You will prosper in the field of wacky inventions."

Alfred laughed. "I think that one was meant for Mr. Pilf."

One thing they all knew for sure was that Mr. Pilf was employed by Merganzer in the field of wacky inventions, though again, no one had the first clue what Pilf was doing there.

"Thank you for all the help, these past months," Alfred said to Bosco. "You've been truly invaluable."

E. J. Bosco had been managing his own hotel, the Boomtown, and the one left by Mr. Pilf, the Spiff, ever since the competition had come to an end.

"I like the Spiff," E. J. Bosco said. "It's no Boomtown, but I whipped it into shape for Mr. Fitzpatrick."

"I'm sure you did. I have high hopes Mr. Fitzpatrick will adequately fill your large shoes."

Alfred looked across the grounds at Fitzpatrick, who, it just so happened, had played a little football back in the day. Alfred thought his old Scottish friend would do a marvelous job with the Spiff Hotel.

"How are things with Lucy?" E. J. Bosco asked. "She fixed the air-conditioning at the Boomtown last week. Did a nice job."

"She's as handy as Leo Fillmore, and that's saying something. Poor Leo is in a losing battle trying to fix everything Remi breaks. I think they're good for each other, don't you?"

They both looked across the pond and saw Lucy, Leo, and Remi tossing bits of bread to a gathering of ducks. Remi started honking like a goofball as Lucy and Leo stole a glance at each other. They were all as happy as could be, and that made both men smile with gladness.

"Looks like it's time for me to get ready," Alfred said. "How's my tie?"

"Ready for what?" E. J. Bosco had no idea what Alfred was talking about, but he straightened the tuxedo's bow tie all the same. "What are you not telling me?"

"Look to the sky and you'll have your answer very soon."

And so E. J. Bosco did look to the sky, and there he saw an airship come suddenly into view. It had been flying secretly overhead for some time, but now its lights were turning on as it came within fifty feet of the grounds.

"Here comes Merganzer!" Remi shouted, and all the guests looked skyward as a rope ladder was tossed overboard.

Captain Rickenbacker, who had been quietly milling about the darker edges of the grounds, appeared behind Mr. Fitzpatrick.

"Cover me. I'm going in."

Captain Rickenbacker loped toward the ladder, trying to be secretive, and then darted behind a bush shaped like a giraffe.

"He's unusual," Fitzpatrick said.

"Par for the course around here," Miss Sheezley felt obligated to say. "You'll get used to it."

"AHOY!" Merganzer called, leaning precariously far over a basket more suited for thirty people than two. "Coming down!"

"Be careful!" Lucy called.

Everyone expected to see Merganzer come down alone, since Mr. Powell would need to man the airship. So they were all surprised when Mr. Powell came down first, followed by Merganzer.

"You didn't leave a monkey in charge up there, did you?" asked Ingrid, the keeper of the jungle under the Whippet Hotel. She was standing with Dr. Flart and Mr. Carp, who were both holding bottles of Flart's Fizz.

"You're looking well, Doctor," Merganzer offered, though really, Flart looked pale as usual. He lived in a dungeon, so it was to be expected. "And you, Mr. Carp, I have need of your services in the field of wacky inventions. We'll talk."

"I'll be ready," Mr. Carp said, his trim mustache wiggling back and forth as he contemplated what madness he might be drawn into next.

Merganzer was tall and Ingrid was short, so he had to lean way down as he took her hand in his and pressed it to his lips.

"Ingrid, charming as usual. We must have tea sometime."

"I bet you say that to all the girls," she said, blushing.

"No, no — only you. The monkeys have been a marvelous help to me these past few months. I couldn't be happier."

This made Ingrid smile, because she trained the orange-tailed Leprechaun monkeys and loved it when her work was appreciated.

"Everyone gather around — they're coming down!" Mr. Powell shouted.

"Who's coming down?" E. J. Bosco asked.

"Who, indeed?" Merganzer said with a wily smile.

A man in a tuxedo started down the rope ladder. Remi, who had come running from the other side of the pond with Leo and Lucy, was the first to shout the man's name.

"Mr. Pilf? What's up, my man?"

"Hello, Remi," Mr. Pilf said, glancing down from the ladder. "What have you been up to?"

"Waiting around for an adventure, mostly. How about you?"

Mr. Pilf reached the ground and brushed off his spiffy black jacket. Everyone moved in close, curious why he was so dolled up.

"Busy," Mr. Pilf said. "In the field of wacky inventions. I work there now, with Merganzer and Powell and the monkeys."

"That's not all he's been up to," Mr. Powell said, his eyes taking to the sky once more.

A small section of the cabin under the blimp disengaged and began moving down. It was a white platform of about four feet by four feet, and as it came closer, everyone saw that someone was standing on top of it.

"Miss Harrington?" Leo and Lucy said simultaneously.

She didn't speak. Instead, she smiled the smile of a bride, which tends to be a special sort of smile. She was wearing a sparkling white dress.

"Well," E. J. Bosco said. "You *have* been busy."

"I've been visiting her on the weekends," Mr. Pilf said. "It just sort of . . . happened, I suppose."

"You were meant for each other," Merganzer added.

Pilar took Mr. Fillmore's hand in hers, remembering her own wedding fondly.

"I love a wedding," she said. "The happiest occasion on earth."

It turned into a magical evening of sparkling lights, lots of dancing, and plenty of laughter. Remi stole the show with his recently acquired break-dancing skills, and Leo and Lucy slow danced for the very first time. Miss Harrington, who was aglow with happiness as the new Mrs. Pilf, threw the bouquet. It was caught by Alfred Whitney, which produced much speculation on the dance floor. It was a night full of magic, and on nights such as those, there is meaning in a thing like catching a bouquet.

"Did you bring Phil?" Lucy asked Merganzer, when it came her turn to dance with the most mysterious man she'd ever known.

"I'm afraid I did not," Merganzer said. He paused for a moment, letting the disappointment really set in. "Would you like to visit him?"

"More than just about anything I can think of," Lucy answered, hoping against all hope.

"Wish granted!" Merganzer said, and seeing the look on her face, he added: "I do so like granting wishes. Very exciting."

The party went on for a little longer, and then Merganzer surprised them all by inviting them on a long weekend to a place they all wanted to go.

"We're all going to the field of wacky inventions — I insist. I've got some new rides to show you. You haven't even tried the Scorpion, Typhoon!, or BLAMMO. The antigravity room is tip-top, ready for another Wyro. And I have new puzzles and games and books and tea."

"I need to see this antigravity business," Captain Rickenbacker said to Mr. Phipps.

"And a new puzzle for us to solve." Mr. Phipps glowed. "We do like a good puzzle, don't we?"

Captain Rickenbacker nodded, then went to the rope ladder to do some reconnaissance work.

"Come along then, it's time we made our way under the cover of darkness."

It was a very Merganzer thing to say. An adventure was afoot, or so it seemed, and danger was in the air.

Everyone boarded together and they flew away into the night sky as one big family. Many hands were held that night on the airship bound for a secret field. Captain Rickenbacker's cape fluttered in the wind and Leo could only imagine what his superhero friend would think of MONDAR. They were a match made in heaven.

Leo leaned over the rail of the cabin and breathed in the cool night air. His two best friends in the whole world stood beside him, and he thought that one day they would all fly so far they might never return. The adventure would only get bigger and more dangerous, until one day, far away in the future, they would vanish into the night sky, to a hotel even Merganzer D. Whippet could not build.

And there they would live on, forever finding new floors to explore and new adventures to be had.

Leo thought this marvelous thought as the wind blew through his thick mop of hair and the airship rose higher and higher on its way to the field of wacky inventions.

And beyond.

Acknowledgments

Trilogies can be a daunting task (fun to start, harder to finish), but they are made less so when I find myself surrounded by talented friends. As we come now to the end of our time in the Whippet Hotel, these people made the task both a joy and a triumph: David Levithan, Lauren Felsenstein, Chris Stengel, Peter Rubie, Susan Schulman (to whom this book is also dedicated), Erin Black, Janet Robbins, and Bess Braswell.

Chris Turnham created whimsically wonderful artwork for the entire series, and Jesse Bernstein brought the audiobooks to life.

For my close friends, who put up with all my Ms. Sparks moments and still decide to keep me around: Skip Pritchard, Mike Wilcox, Jeff Green, Jeremy Gonzalez, Jeffrey Townsend, Marcus Wilcox, Matt McKern, and Squire Broel.

Fellow friends who are also authors and know the sharp curves and exhausting moments along the way — David Shannon and Jon Scieszka.

For moms — Remy and Oma — you always read my books and say nice things, and that's 100 percent of what is hoped for. Hugs.

And above all to Reece Carman, for her boundless imagination and big heart. She made the Whippet Hotel possible. She really did. XOXO.